SCRIPT BY
PAUL TOBIN

ART, COLORS, AND LETTERS BY
RON CHAN

COVER BY
RON CHAN

EARTH BOY *CREATED BY:*
PAUL TOBIN AND RON CHAN

DARK HORSE BOOKS

PRESIDENT & PUBLISHER MIKE RICHARDSON EDITOR DANIEL CHABON ASSISTANT EDITOR CHUCK HOWITT
DESIGNER ETHAN KIMBERLING DIGITAL ART TECHNICIAN ANN GRAY

EARTH BOY

Collects the Dark Horse Comics original graphic novel *Earth Boy*.

Published by
Dark Horse Books
A division of Dark Horse Comics LLC
10956 SE Main Street
Milwaukie, OR 97222

DarkHorse.com

To find a comics shop in your area, visit
comicshoplocator.com

First Edition: March 2021
Ebook ISBN 978-1-50671-417-2
Trade Paperback ISBN 978-1-50671-411-0

10 9 8 7 6 5 4 3 2 1
Printed in China

EARTH: APRIL 7, 3115.
GALACTIC RANGER BENSON CHOW STARES INTO THE FACE OF DEATH ITSELF!

MUNCH
CHOMP CHOMP

THROUGHOUT THE COSMOS, NO DEADLIER BEAST EXISTS THAN THE M'OO C'OW KNOWN AS BETSY!
IT WAS SHE THAT BROUGHT ABOUT THE END OF THE TRI-PLANET FEDERATION!
IT WAS SHE WHO TRIGGERED THE GREAT LETHAL PULSE THAT WROUGHT DEVASTATION ACROSS UNTOLD GALAXIES!
IT WAS THIS HORRIBLE BEAST, THIS UNSTOPPABLE COSMIC CYCLONE OF DESTRUCTION, THAT CAUSED THE ERA OF NINE BILLION WEEPING MOTHERS, AND...

URF!!

HMM. WANT IN ON THIS? NO PROBLEM.

AND SO, ACCOMPANIED BY HIS FAITHFUL SIDEKICK, MR. BITTLES, AND LAUGHING IN THE FACE OF ALMOST CERTAIN ANNIHILATION...
...GALACTIC RANGER CHOW ACTIVATES HUMANITY'S LAST HOPE, A MACHINE THAT CAN DRAIN THE MURDEROUS MILK OF M'OO C'OW AND...
MILK-N' MASTER 4000

YO! BENSON!

KENJI? WHAT BRINGS YOU AROUND?
THOUGHT I'D SEE IF YOU COULD HANG OUT TODAY. WAS THINKIN' 'BOUT GOING INTO TOWN.

NAWW. I GOT TOO MANY CHORES.
DANG. WELL... LEAST LET ME SHOW YOU SOMETHING INCREDIBLY AMAZING THAT WILL CHANGE THE VERY MANNER IN WHICH YOU SEE THE WORLD.

WHAT IS IT?
COME AROUND THIS WAY.

CHECK IT OUT!
I GOT ME A NEW SET OF JETS!

BARK!
CLANK!!
BARK!

WELL. NEW JETS FOR ME, ANYWAY. DAD SAYS IF I CAN KEEP IT RUNNING, IT'S MINE.
SURE YOU CAN'T GO FOR A SPIN? WE HAVE LADIES TO VAGUELY IMPRESS!

I REALLY CAN'T. IT'S A **HUGE** CHORE DAY. AND WITH SIS GONE TO HER SWIM MEET, I HAVE TO DO EVERYTHING MYSELF.
NOBODY EVER **HAS** TO DO EVERYTHING BY THEMSELVES WHEN THEY HAVE **AMAZING** FRIENDS.
YOU GOT ANY?

KENJI, WOULD YOU--
BE **GLAD** TO HELP! NOT A PROBLEM.
BUT YOU HAVE TO TELL YOUR SISTER THAT I GLISTEN IN THE SUN.

I'LL TELL HER YOU DON'T STINK MUCH. HOW'S THAT?
I'LL **TAKE** IT.
GOTTA BUILD A FOUNDATION SOMEWHERE.
LEAD-R

AN HOUR LATER...

SO... I HAVE TO ASK, WHEN I WAS WALKING UP ON YOU, I COULD HEAR YOU TALKING TO YOURSELF AND SOUNDING...
I'M TRYING TO BE NICE HERE...
COMPLETELY INSANE.
WHAT WAS THAT ALL ABOUT?

I MEAN, YOU STILL DREAMING OF THAT SPACE RANGER STUFF?
KINDA DUMB, ISN'T IT?

IT'S NOT DUMB! THE KAYRUS GALACTIC RANGER ACADEMY IS LEGENDARY!
IT GOES BACK ALMOST A HUNDRED AND TWENTY THOUSAND YEARS!

"THE GALACTIC RANGERS PATROL THE ENTIRETY OF THE KNOWN UNIVERSE!

"SOME OF THE UNIVERSE'S GREATEST LEGENDS GRADUATED FROM THE KAYRUS ACADEMY! KANNON JRLL OF MOLDERON SEVEN! DRRG OF PENN! THE BROKEN BROTHERS OF THE FOG! EVEN LITTLE PEG OF THE NEG-LIGHT SYSTEM!

"IT WAS THE KAYRUS ACADEMY THAT TRAINED **ALL** OF THEM, AS WELL AS THOUSANDS OF **OTHERS** WHO FIGHT TO MAKE THE UNIVERSE A BETTER PLACE!

"AT THE KAYRUS ACADEMY, YOU LEARN HOW TO FLY **SPACESHIPS**!

"AND YOU IMMERSE YOURSELF IN **ALIEN** CULTURES! MINGLING WITH CADETS FROM ALL ACROSS THE KNOWN UNIVERSE!

"YOU LEARN GALACTIC PHILOSOPHY!"

AND THERE'S A MASSIVE AMOUNT OF COMBAT TRAINING, BECAUSE YOU NEVER KNOW WHO YOU'LL RUN UP AGAINST WHEN YOU'RE A GALACTIC RANGER!
PAFF!!
BARK!
BARK!!

"AND OF COURSE YOU LEARN SPACE SCIENCE, BECAUSE A RANGER WITH A **PISTOL** CAN ONLY SOLVE **SOME** PROBLEMS, BUT A RANGER WITH A **BRAIN** CAN SOLVE THEM **ALL**."

AND THAT'S ONLY THE TIP OF THE ICEBERG! THE KAYRUS ACADEMY TRAINS YOU IN **HUNDREDS** OF DIFFERENT AREAS!
IF YOU'RE A GALACTIC RANGER, THEN--

BENSON! **COOL** IT! I **UNDERSTAND**!

I WASN'T SAYING THE KAYRUS ACADEMY IS DUMB.
I WAS SAYING... I JUST MEANT... UH... YOU KNOW.

I KNOW **WHAT**?
WELL... IT'S JUST THAT... C'MON, BEN. YOU **KNOW** WHAT I'M SAYING.

NOBODY FROM EARTH HAS **EVER** BEEN ACCEPTED INTO THE KAYRUS ACADEMY. **EVER**.
WE'RE TOO NEW OF A PLANET! TOO MUCH OF A FRONTIER OUTPOST!
IT'S **NOT** GONNA HAPPEN!

YOU'RE ALWAYS THINKING ABOUT THAT KAYRUS PLACE, BUT IT'S IN THE ANDROMEDA SEVENTEEN GALAXY!
THAT'S LIKE, **WAY** OVER A **MEGA-PARSEC** AWAY! YOU **AIN'T** GOING!

HARDLY **ANYONE** GETS TO LEAVE THE GALAXY! YOU **BELONG** HERE! ON **EARTH**! ON THIS **FARM**!
YOU'RE **GREAT** WITH ALL THE ANIMALS! HORSES! COWS! DOGS! MARS RAPTORS! **ANYTHING**!

LOOK! THOSE THINGS EAT RIGHT OUT OF YOUR HANDS!
BUT IF **I** GET TOO CLOSE, THEY'LL BITE FIRST AND ASK QUESTIONS LATER, AFTER **POOPING** ME OUT IN THE MEANTIME!

I MEAN... IT'S NOT SO BAD, HERE, IS IT?
NO. IT AIN'T. I LOVE IT.

BUT... I... I DUNNO. IT'S SO **BIG** OUT THERE. I WANNA SEE IT, I GUESS.
SOMETIMES IT DOESN'T MATTER WHAT YOU WANT.
SORRY. THAT'S JUST THE TRUTH OF IT.

LISTEN. I GOTTA FIRE UP THOSE NEW JETS OF MINE. YOU SURE YOU DON'T WANT TO COME ALONG FOR A RIDE?
CAN'T. I STILL HAVE TO WATER THE PIGS AND THE BABY MARS MAMMOTHS.
COOL, COOL. SOON, THOUGH. SEE YOU LATER.

DON'T FORGET TO TELL YOUR SISTER I SAID HELLO!

I AM GOOD WITH ANIMALS.
RRRF!

pant
pant
pant

UP TOP!
SNAP!
LEAP!

SIT!
SNAP!
PLOP

ROLL OVER!
SNAP!
twirl!

THUMP!

THAT ONE WAS MY BAD.
RUFF!

BENSON? CAN YOU COME BACK TO THE HOUSE FOR A BIT?

HEY, DAD. I'M ALMOST DONE WITH CHORES. ANY WORD FROM LILA?
SHE WON. NEW RECORD. NOT SURE HOW I FATHERED A SWIMMER.

SHE'S JUST DEDICATED. THAT'S HOW YOU RAISED US. WHATEVER DIRECTION A CHOW FACES, GO FULL SPEED, RIGHT?
I SUPPOSE. AS LONG AS YOU'RE HAVING FUN, TOO. THAT'S IMPORTANT.

SO... I WANTED TO TALK TO YOU ABOUT SOMETHING. THIS CAME IN THE MAIL TODAY.
IT'S FROM THE **KAYRUS ACADEMY**.
WHAT?! I NEVER THOUGHT THEY'D ACTUALLY **ANSWER**! WHAT DOES IT--

I ALREADY OPENED IT. AND READ THE LETTER.
SIT DOWN, BENSON.
BUT, WHAT DOES IT--

BENSON, YOU'VE ALWAYS BEEN A DREAMER. THAT'S WHAT I WANT TO TALK TO YOU ABOUT.
YOU NEED TO UNDERSTAND THAT, SOMETIMES, DREAMS END.
OH. OKAY. UHH.
AHH, OKAY.

WHICH IS CENTERED IN THE GREAT HELM, THE FIRST GALAXY CREATED BY INTELLIGENT BEINGS.

YOU BECOME A **MAN** THE FIRST TIME YOU PUT ASIDE YOUR DAYDREAMS AND TRY TO MAKE THEM REALITY, **GUIDING** YOUR FATE INSTEAD OF SIMPLY **DREAMING** ABOUT IT.

... YOU MAKE NEW ONES.

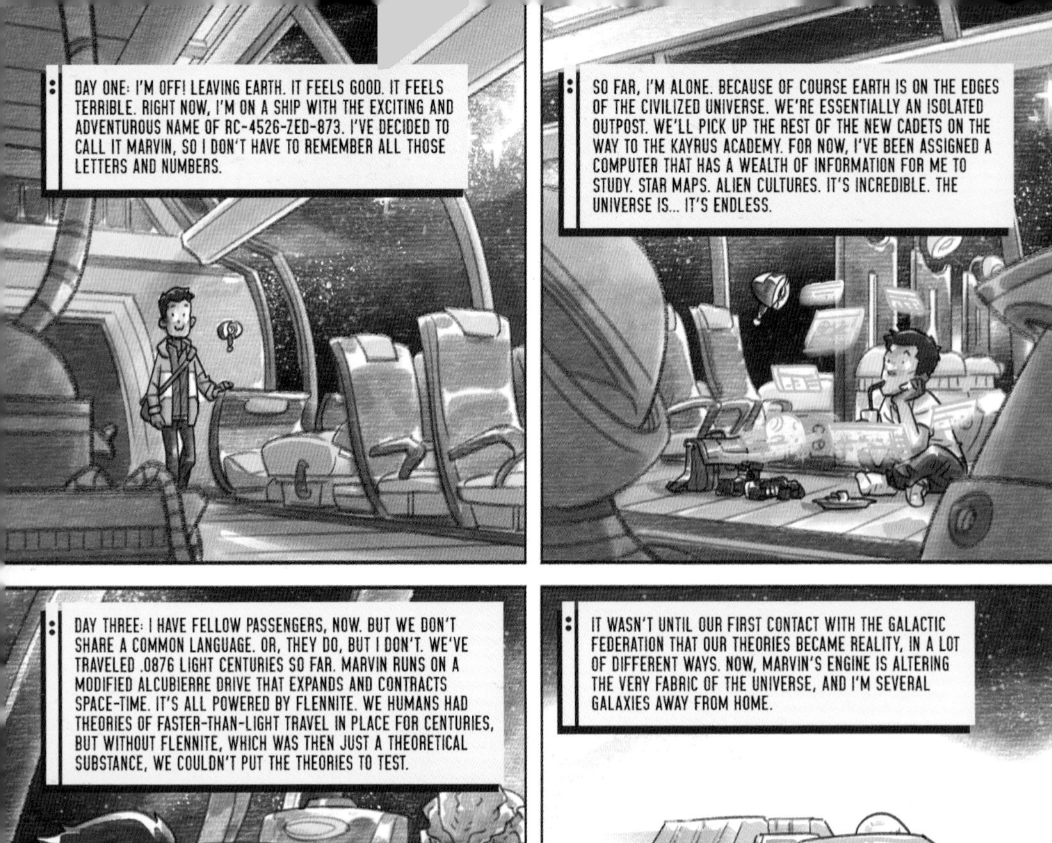
DAY ONE: I'M OFF! LEAVING EARTH. IT FEELS GOOD. IT FEELS TERRIBLE. RIGHT NOW, I'M ON A SHIP WITH THE EXCITING AND ADVENTUROUS NAME OF RC-4526-ZED-873. I'VE DECIDED TO CALL IT MARVIN, SO I DON'T HAVE TO REMEMBER ALL THOSE LETTERS AND NUMBERS.
SO FAR, I'M ALONE. BECAUSE OF COURSE EARTH IS ON THE EDGES OF THE CIVILIZED UNIVERSE. WE'RE ESSENTIALLY AN ISOLATED OUTPOST. WE'LL PICK UP THE REST OF THE NEW CADETS ON THE WAY TO THE KAYRUS ACADEMY. FOR NOW, I'VE BEEN ASSIGNED A COMPUTER THAT HAS A WEALTH OF INFORMATION FOR ME TO STUDY. STAR MAPS. ALIEN CULTURES. IT'S INCREDIBLE. THE UNIVERSE IS... IT'S ENDLESS.

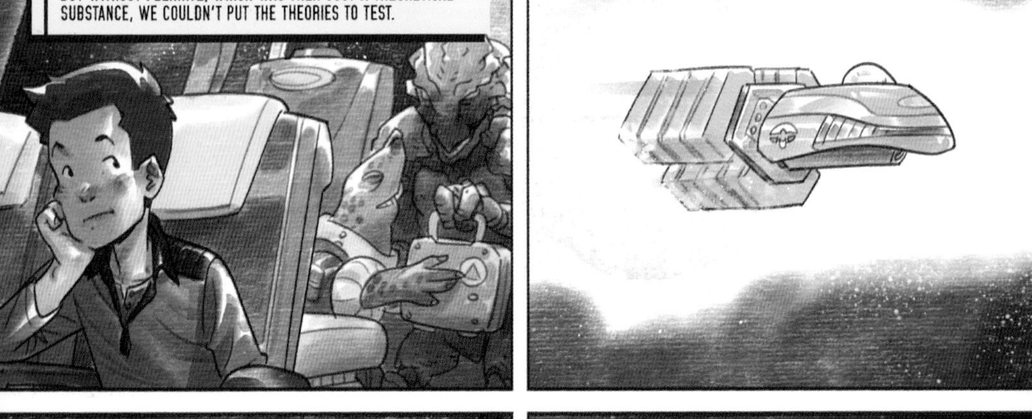
DAY THREE: I HAVE FELLOW PASSENGERS, NOW. BUT WE DON'T SHARE A COMMON LANGUAGE. OR, THEY DO, BUT I DON'T. WE'VE TRAVELED .0876 LIGHT CENTURIES SO FAR. MARVIN RUNS ON A MODIFIED ALCUBIERRE DRIVE THAT EXPANDS AND CONTRACTS SPACE-TIME. IT'S ALL POWERED BY FLENNITE. WE HUMANS HAD THEORIES OF FASTER-THAN-LIGHT TRAVEL IN PLACE FOR CENTURIES, BUT WITHOUT FLENNITE, WHICH WAS THEN JUST A THEORETICAL SUBSTANCE, WE COULDN'T PUT THE THEORIES TO TEST.
IT WASN'T UNTIL OUR FIRST CONTACT WITH THE GALACTIC FEDERATION THAT OUR THEORIES BECAME REALITY, IN A LOT OF DIFFERENT WAYS. NOW, MARVIN'S ENGINE IS ALTERING THE VERY FABRIC OF THE UNIVERSE, AND I'M SEVERAL GALAXIES AWAY FROM HOME.

MARVIN'S HULL IS MADE OF TRIBIUM, OF COURSE. IT'S THE ONLY SUBSTANCE THAT CAN WITHSTAND THIS TYPE OF TRAVEL. THE FLENNITE FUEL IS INCREDIBLY RARE. TRIBIUM IS EVEN MORE SCARCE. IN FACT, IT'S PRETTY MUCH USED UP, THESE DAYS, FAR TOO RARE TO CONSTRUCT ANY MORE SHIPS, EVEN IF THERE WAS ANY SURPLUS OF FLENNITE TO FUEL THEM. THE GREAT AGE OF SPACE TRAVEL IS FINISHED.
OF COURSE, LIGHT CENTURIES OF SPACE HAVE ALREADY BEEN EXPLORED, BUT WITH THE SEVERELY DIMINISHED RESERVES OF FLENNITE AND TRIBIUM, THERE'S STILL... INFINITE UNIVERSE OUT THERE. USUALLY I'M FASCINATED BY ANY THOUGHTS OF THE INFINITE, BUT TODAY I'M TRYING NOT TO THINK ABOUT IT. I ALREADY FEEL PRETTY SMALL.

DAY SIX: GREAT. AFTER ALMOST A WEEK OF TRAVEL I JUST LEARNED THAT MY COMPUTER, WHICH I'VE NAMED CHESHIRE, CAN TRANSLATE BACK AND FORTH BETWEEN ALMOST ANY LANGUAGE. I COULD'VE BEEN TALKING TO THE OTHERS THIS WHOLE TIME.

BY NOW THEY'RE ALL AVOIDING ME, THOUGH, BECAUSE THEY THOUGHT I WAS BEING RUDE FOR THE PAST FEW DAYS. I'D FEEL WORSE ABOUT IT, BUT, REALLY, THERE'S TOO MUCH TO DISTRACT ME. WE'RE NEARING THE KAYRUS ACADEMY. IT'S ONLY ABOUT TWO LIGHT DAYS AHEAD, NOW.

WE'VE STARTED TO SEE SIGNS. THEY APPEAR AT ALL THE COORDINATION POINTS THAT OUR FTL DRIVES LOCK ONTO, THE AREAS OF SPACE THAT CAN'T BE FOLDED BY OUR ALCUBIERRE DRIVE. AND THERE'S OCCASIONAL TRAFFIC, NOW. OTHER SHIPS.

DAY SEVEN: WE JUST PASSED BY A THAGLIAN SHIP. IT'S *INCREDIBLY* MASSIVE. THE SIZE OF A MOON. DESPITE ITS SIZE, CHESHIRE TOLD ME THAT IT'S ONLY A TWO-PERSON VESSEL. SO--SERIOUSLY? THERE'S ONLY ROOM IN THAT THING FOR *TWO* THAGLIANS? THEY MUST BE *HUGE*. THE UNIVERSE IS SO STRANGE. SO EXCITING.

DAY EIGHT: THERE IT IS! I'VE SEEN IT BEFORE, IN THE MOVIES AND... JUST *EVERYWHERE*. IT'S *KAYRUS*. SERIOUSLY. I CAN'T BELIEVE THIS. THERE IT IS. *IT'S RIGHT THERE.*

AND HERE I AM.

I'M HERE.

I'M INSTANTLY LOST. IT'S LIKE A FOREST OF INCREDIBLY ADVANCED TECHNOLOGY AND AMAZINGLY DIVERSE ALIENS. AND THAT'S FINE, BECAUSE I LOVE EXPLORING IN THE FOREST.

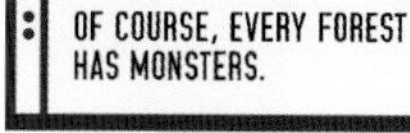
OF COURSE, EVERY FOREST HAS MONSTERS.

THOKK!
UNFFF!

THERE, STUCKERS. YOU OWE ME TEN CREDITS. YOU SHOULDN'T HAVE BET ME I WOULDN'T PUNCH THE BIGGEST LOSER IN SIGHT.
OH, I KNEW YOU'D DO IT, SPRATT, BUT I FIGURED IT WAS WORTH THE CREDITS TO WATCH.
WAIT A SECOND, THAT'S THE KID FROM EARTH.

SERIOUSLY? IT'S THE GNAT?
HEY, LOSER, WE STUDIED EARTH FOR LIKE, TWO SECONDS IN OUR IMPORTANT PLANETS COURSE. YOU KNOW WHY?
BECAUSE THAT'S HOW LONG IT TAKES TO SAY, "EARTH ISN'T IMPORTANT."

LATER, AFTER THEY'RE GONE, CHESHIRE TELLS ME ALL ABOUT THE FIRST CADETS TO WELCOME ME TO THE KAYRUS ACADEMY. SPRATT, STUCKERS, AND LOWENGEAR. ALL THREE OF THEM ARE "LEGACY" STUDENTS, MEANING THEY RECEIVED SCHOLARSHIPS DUE TO HAVING HAD RELATIVES GRADUATE WITH HIGH HONORS.

EVEN SO, IT TOOK A SIZABLE DONATION FOR SPRATT TO RECEIVE ADMISSION. ALL THREE OF THEM ARE FROM WEALTHY FAMILIES, THOUGH, AND WHEN SPACE IS INVOLVED, WEALTH CAN BE VAST. STUCKERS'S DAD OWNS PLANETS. LIKE, MULTIPLE PLANETS. CHESHIRE TELLS ME HE'S A TOTALLY CRAPPY LANDLORD, THOUGH.

CHESHIRE ALSO TELLS ME THAT GUY WHO WAS WATCHING, THE ONE WITH THE SMIRK, WAS WEARING A TEACHER'S BADGE. SO, THAT'S JUST EXCELLENT.

I'LL BE ROOMING WITH A GUY NAMED BOGLEY. HE SEEMS COOL. REMINDS ME OF KENJI, ACTUALLY. HE SMELLS LIKE A BEACH AND HIS VOICE IS THIS REALLY COOL RUMBLE, LIKE A MERMAID GARGLING. THAT DOESN'T MAKE IT SOUND AS COOL AS IT ACTUALLY IS.

RIGHT? IT'S INCREDIBLE. I HOPE WE'LL HAVE TIME FOR SOME SWIMMING. I WONDER WHAT LIVES BENEATH THOSE WAVES. I HEAR SOME STUDENTS ARE FULLY AQUATIC. I BET THEY HAVE DORMS DOWN THERE.

DAY TEN: THE PLAN FOR TODAY IS JUST TO WALK AROUND. I'VE LEARNED HOW TO SAY "HELLO" AND "THANKS" IN GALACTIC. THE LANGUAGE IS REALLY EASY. I GUESS IT WOULD HAVE TO BE, SEEING AS HOW IT NEEDS TO BE SPOKEN BY SUCH A HUGE RANGE OF PEOPLE, LIKE... GAS FORMS, FISH, BY PEOPLE WITH *NO* TONGUES, OR PEOPLE WITH *FIVE* TONGUES.

MY ADVISOR'S NAME IS PRINN. SHE'S THE KAYRUS ACADEMY'S *ONLY* EARTH-CERTIFIED TEACHER. ONLY ONE, OUT OF OVER THREE THOUSAND TEACHERS. INCREDIBLE.

SO, MY ADMISSION PAPERS AREN'T READY YET?

NOT QUITE YET. SHOULD BE SOON. DON'T LET IT BOTHER YOU. PAPERWORK CAN TAKE FOREVER, SOMETIMES.

I MANAGE TO MAKE A FOOL OF MYSELF BY TALKING TO A BRESSIAN'S PET, THINKING *IT* WAS THE BRESSIAN. TURNS OUT, BRESSIANS LOOK LIKE MY SISTER LILA'S PARAKEET, AND RIDE AROUND ON THEIR PETS. STUPID ME, FOR ASSUMING THE OPPOSITE. LOTS OF PEOPLE LAUGHED AT ME. THE BRESSIAN WAS MAD. I GUESS I WOULD BE, TOO. FROM HER SIDE, IT WAS PROBABLY INSULTING. FROM MINE, IT WAS EMBARRASSING.

I HUNG OUT NEAR THE HEROES MONUMENT FOR A TIME. SO STRANGE TO ACTUALLY TOUCH THE REAL STATUES I'VE SEEN IN SO MANY MOVIES. I STARED AT THEM FOR A LONG TIME, TRYING TO REMEMBER THAT *THEY* WEREN'T PERFECT EITHER.

CULTURAL TENSIONS ARE INEVITABLE IN SPACE. LITTLE PEG OF THE NEG-LIGHT SYSTEM ONCE NEARLY ENDED THE VESERIN TREATY-ALLIANCE WHEN SHE FORGOT TO ROTATE TWICE BEFORE PUTTING HER FOOT IN THE SPEECH POOL. IT MIGHT SEEM SILLY TO US, BUT IT WAS A GRAVE INSULT TO THE PEOPLE OF VESERIN.

DAY ELEVEN: FOOD HAS BEEN . . . INTERESTING.
FIND ANYTHING YOU LIKE? THE FOODS SHOULD BE SUBCATEGORIZED ACCORDING TO YOUR DNA HELIX, CROSS-REFERENCED BY YOUR TASTE BUDS, DIGESTIVE SYSTEM PREFERENCES, AND CAPABILITIES.
YOU KNOW, BOGLEY, I THINK I'VE SEEN MATHEMATICAL EXPLANATIONS FOR THE **UNIVERSE** THAT ARE SIMPLER THAN THIS MENU.

MADE NEW FRIENDS TODAY! *THE EMILY TWINS*. EMILY LORNA AND EMILY SORAYA. THEY'RE FROM THE BURROWS SYSTEM. IT'S MOSTLY GAS GIANT PLANETS THERE, ACCORDING TO CHESHIRE.
I AGREE WITH BENSON. THERE SHOULD BE A FULL SEMESTER COURSE ON HOW TO READ THAT MENU!

SO, WHY DO THEY CALL YOU **TWINS**?
DUH. BECAUSE WE'RE PRACTICALLY **IDENTICAL**, BENSON! HARDLY **ANYONE** CAN TELL US APART.
IT'S FUN PRETENDING TO BE MY SISTER, FOOLING EVERYBODY.

I DON'T GET IT. YOU TWO DON'T LOOK ANYTHING ALIKE.
LOOK ALIKE? YOU MEAN WITH, LIKE, **EYESIGHT**? WHAT'S THAT EVEN MATTER?
OUR SCENTS AND WING VIBRATION SPEEDS HAVE IDENTICAL SIGNATURES. WE'RE TWINS!

SORAYA ACTUALLY THOUGHT I WAS JOKING ABOUT BEING ABLE TO TELL THEM APART. THEY KEPT SWITCHING CHAIRS TO FOOL US. BOGLEY WAS FOOLED ABOUT HALF THE TIME, EVEN THOUGH HE WAS PAYING ATTENTION. AS FOR ME, I GUESS I'M LEARNING THAT ALIEN CULTURES ARE MORE THAN JUST PEOPLE WHO LOOK DIFFERENT; THEY HAVE ENTIRELY DIFFERENT WAYS OF THINKING AND PERCEIVING THE UNIVERSE.
OKAY. WHICH OF US IS WHICH? GUESS!

THE UNIVERSE IS EVEN MORE INFINITE THAN I THOUGHT.

DAY TWELVE: DEDICATING THIS DAY TO FRIENDS AND FAMILY.
KENJI? IT'S ME, BENSON! I FINALLY HAVE A TURN AT THE TACHYON PULSE PHONE.
MY REGULAR PHONE WOULD TAKE SEVENTEEN CENTURIES BETWEEN TRANSMISSIONS, SO I'M USING THIS ONE, SINCE I KNOW YOU PROBABLY HAVE CHORES TO DO.

UH-HUH, YEAH, BLAH BLAH BLAH. COOL TO TALK WITH YOU AGAIN, BENSON, BUT CUT TO THE CHASE.
TELL ME ABOUT ALL THOSE CADET GIRLS! ARE THEY BEAUTIFUL? AND THE CARS! ARE THEY FAST?

OH, YOU WOULDN'T BELIEVE THE GIRLS HERE!
LIKE, HONESTLY AND SERIOUSLY... YOU WOULDN'T BELIEVE THE GIRLS HERE.
AND THE CARS HERE MAKE THAT OLD JUNKER OF YOURS LOOK LIKE... UHH... WELL I GUESS IT COULDN'T LOOK ANY WORSE.

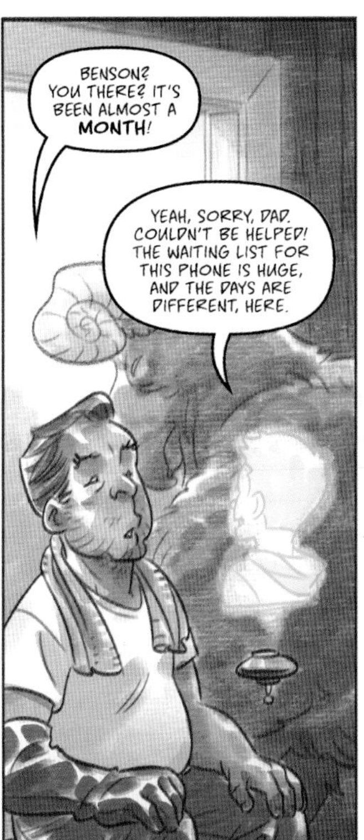
BENSON? YOU THERE? IT'S BEEN ALMOST A MONTH!
YEAH, SORRY, DAD. COULDN'T BE HELPED! THE WAITING LIST FOR THIS PHONE IS HUGE, AND THE DAYS ARE DIFFERENT, HERE.

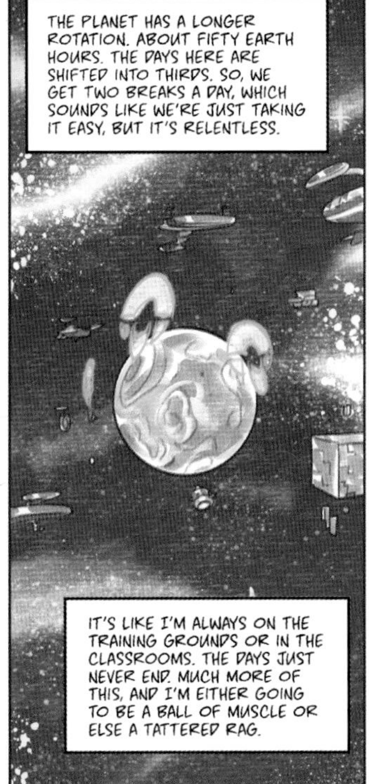
THE PLANET HAS A LONGER ROTATION. ABOUT FIFTY EARTH HOURS. THE DAYS HERE ARE SHIFTED INTO THIRDS. SO, WE GET TWO BREAKS A DAY, WHICH SOUNDS LIKE WE'RE JUST TAKING IT EASY, BUT IT'S RELENTLESS.
IT'S LIKE I'M ALWAYS ON THE TRAINING GROUNDS OR IN THE CLASSROOMS. THE DAYS JUST NEVER END. MUCH MORE OF THIS, AND I'M EITHER GOING TO BE A BALL OF MUSCLE OR ELSE A TATTERED RAG.

YOU'LL MAKE IT. YOU'VE ALWAYS HAD MORE THAN ENOUGH PASSION FOR A HUNDRED-HOUR DAY, LET ALONE SOME LITTLE FIFTY-HOUR THING.
I'LL TELL LILA YOU CALLED. AND, PUT YOUR NAME ON THE PHONE LIST AGAIN, RIGHT AWAY. TRY TO CALL MORE OFTEN. WE MISS YOU.
MR. BITTLES SAYS HELLO.
URFF!

DAY FIFTEEN: JUST GREAT.
UNHH!

WHAT A STUPID BONE STRUCTURE. ARE ALL EARTH PEOPLE LIKE YOU, OR ARE YOU JUST THE MOST PATHETIC GNAT THERE, TOO?
I BET EARTH JUST SENT YOU HERE TO GET RID OF YOU.
WHAT'S GOING ON HERE?

OH, UH, DIRECTOR SQUA-TRONT. THE EARTH BOY ATTACKED US.
WE WERE JUST STANDING HERE, AND HE LEAPT OUT AT US, WITH HIS FANGS OUT, SMELLING OF PEE AND SCREAMING ABOUT HATING THE GALACTIC FEDERATION.

HMM. WELL, HE LOOKS TO HAVE LEARNED HIS LESSON.
YOU LEARN YOUR LESSON, BOY?
UH, YES, SIR.

WHY DIDN'T YOU TELL ON THEM?
WELL, FOR ONE, THEY JUMPED ME ON MY WAY TO THE TRAINING COURSE, AND IN A WAY THEY'RE ACTUALLY HELPING TRAIN ME TO FIGHT. A LITTLE. MAYBE.
BUT, MOSTLY, I CAN'T JUST GO RUNNING FOR HELP. HOW CAN I BE A GALACTIC RANGER IF I CAN'T HANDLE A FEW BULLIES?

DAY TWENTY: BEEN TAKING A LOT OF EVALUATION TESTS THE PAST WEEK.

THE THEME IS... HOW WOULD YOU SURVIVE IF YOU CRASH-LANDED ON A PRIMITIVE ALIEN PLANET, WITH NO SUPPLIES, NO ACCESS TO COMPUTERS, NO *NOTHING*?

UNFORTUNATELY, SINCE ALL WE CAN HAVE IS A PENCIL AND PAPER FOR THE TESTS, THAT MEANS I DON'T HAVE ACCESS TO CHESHIRE, WHICH IN TURN MEANS...

... EVERYTHING IS INCOMPREHENSIBLE. EVERYONE ELSE IS DOING FINE. I'M THE ONLY ONE WHO DOESN'T SPEAK ANY OF THE LANGUAGES, NOT EVEN THE COMMON GALACTIC.
YOU SHOULD KNOW **ALL ABOUT** PRIMITIVE PLANETS, SINCE YOU'RE **FROM** ONE.

YOU SHOULD HAVE JUST MARKED **SOMETHING**! I MEAN, IF YOU FILLED IN **A** OR **B** OR **C**, YOU'D HAVE GOTTEN LIKE, A THIRD OF THE ANSWERS RIGHT, JUST BY CHANCE!
I SUPPOSE. BUT, WHY? I'M NOT HERE TO GET GOOD TEST SCORES. I'M HERE TO LEARN.

SO IF I DON'T KNOW THE ANSWERS, WHY FAKE IT? I DON'T LEARN ANYTHING THAT WAY.
I'M NOT WORRIED ABOUT THE TESTS. I'LL LEARN GALACTIC. I'LL LEARN ANYTHING I NEED TO LEARN. IT'S JUST MORE STUDYING TO DO. THE ACADEMY BELIEVES IN ME, AND THAT GIVES ME STRENGTH.

DAY TWENTY-THREE: FITTING IN. KIND OF. A LITTLE.

BENSON! IT'S SORAYA! ME AND LORNA AND BOGLEY ARE AT THE CASTAWAY CAFE! THEY HAVE GRIBBLEGRAM-FLAVORED ICE CREAM! NONE OF US EVEN KNOW WHAT THAT IS! COME JOIN US!
CAN DO! I'M ON THE WAY!

SOMETIMES WHEN I'M WALKING, I TURN OFF CHESHIRE. OR AT LEAST DON'T LET HER TRANSLATE THE CROWD AROUND ME. IT CAN HURT, SOMETIMES, TO LISTEN.
THERE IT IS. DON'T GET TOO CLOSE.
HEARD IT ATTACKED SOME BOYS ON THE TRAINING COURSE.
IT'S HIDEOUS. DARE YOU TO TOUCH IT.
... A STAIN ON THE ACADEMY TO EVEN LET SOMETHING LIKE THAT THROUGH THE DOORS.

SO THIS IS GRIBBLEGRAM? WHAT IS IT?
SOME KIND OF BERRY FROM THE WHIRLPOOL GALAXY. TASTES A LITTLE LIKE CHELLIC, I THINK. OR MAYBE TUMSQUDGE?
I HAVE NO IDEA WHAT EITHER OF THOSE THINGS ARE, BUT THEY MUST BE DELICIOUS!

SIS! IT'S ME. I GOT PHONE PRIVILEGES AGAIN.
SORAYA GAVE ME HER TURN, SINCE HER PARENTS ARE TRAVELING OUT OF RANGE ANYWAY, AND HER SISTER IS ALREADY HERE.

OH-HO! WHO'S THIS SORAYA GIRL WHO'S DOING AWESOME FAVORS FOR YOU?
OH, JUST A FRIEND. LIKE, ONE OF VERY FEW I HAVE. THREE, ACTUALLY. SORAYA, AND HER SISTER LORNA, AND THEN MY DORM MATE, BOGLEY. THEY'RE ALL GREAT!

THEY'RE KIND OF OUTCASTS, THOUGH, I GUESS, AND I DEFINITELY AM, SO IT'S LIKE ONLY THE OUTCASTS WILL TALK TO ME.

UH-HUH. I'M WEEPING, OVER HERE. JUST WEEPING.
LISTEN, BENSON, SOUNDS TO ME AS IF YOU LIKE YOUR THREE FRIENDS MORE THAN ANYONE ELSE, AND SINCE YOU'RE ALREADY FRIENDS WITH THEM, IT SEEMS LIKE EVERYTHING'S WORKING OUT, AND YOU SHOULDN'T BE SUCH A BRAT.

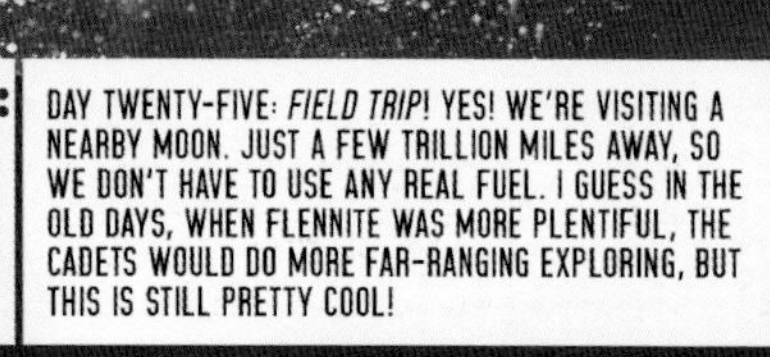

DAY TWENTY-FIVE: *FIELD TRIP*! YES! WE'RE VISITING A NEARBY MOON. JUST A FEW TRILLION MILES AWAY, SO WE DON'T HAVE TO USE ANY REAL FUEL. I GUESS IN THE OLD DAYS, WHEN FLENNITE WAS MORE PLENTIFUL, THE CADETS WOULD DO MORE FAR-RANGING EXPLORING, BUT THIS IS STILL PRETTY COOL!

OUR SHIP IS PILOTED BY AN UPPER-CLASSMAN. A SIXTH YEAR CADET NAMED *PILO*. SHE'S AN ABAGRASSIAN. REALLY NICE. HER FOURTH EYE CAN APPARENTLY SEE IN FIVE DIMENSIONS, INCLUDING TIME ITSELF, SO SHE SAYS WE BETTER NOT TRY TO MISBEHAVE, OR SHE'LL CATCH US *FOR SURE*.
LORNA, TWELVE MINUTES FROM NOW, DON'T EVEN THINK ABOUT IT!

BOGLEY IS SCANNING EVERYTHING HE CAN, GETTING ALL SORTS OF REFERENCE DATA FOR HIS GAME. WHENEVER HE AIMS HIS SPHERE MY WAY, I TRY TO LOOK REALLY NOBLE AND STRONG, SO I DON'T END UP AS SOME DORKY VILLAGE IDIOT, ASSUMING HE EVEN PUTS ME IN THE GAME.

THE EMILY TWINS GET TO TRY A SPACEWALK ON THE WAY TO KIRBYUN, THE MOON. SORAYA TOLD ME THAT WHEN SHE'S OUTSIDE A SHIP, SHE CAN HEAR THE UNIVERSE'S MUSIC BETTER. IT WOULD BE *AMAZING* TO HEAR THAT KIND OF MUSIC. WHAT A CHANGE OF PERSPECTIVE THAT WOULD BE! IT'S FASCINATING TO LEARN ABOUT ALIENS. ESPECIALLY SORAYA. I FEEL LIKE I'VE KNOWN HER FOREVER.

COME OUTSIDE! BENSON, COME OUT HERE!
NO, BENSON, YOU STAY.
AND YOU GIRLS GET IN HERE. WE'RE APPROACHING LOW ORBIT.

KIRBYUN TURNS OUT TO BE A DUSTY MOON.
FWOOF!

LIKE, *SERIOUSLY* DUSTY.
PUFF
PUFF
PUFF

OKAY! WE'RE DOING TETHER EXERCISES, SO LINK UP WITH A PARTNER, AND WE'LL RUN THROUGH SOME LOW-GRAVITY EXPLORATION TECHNIQUES!

WE'LL BE USING LEVEL-FIVE ENERGY COUPLERS FOR TETHERS. THEY EXPAND AND CONTRACT AS NEEDED.
DON'T MOVE AROUND TOO MUCH UNTIL YOU'RE USED TO THE GRAVITATIONAL DIFFERENCES, AND YOUR PARTNER IS USED TO ANCHORING YOUR WEIGHT.
THINK OF IT LIKE ROCK CLIMBING, EXCEPT THAT IT'S NOT AT ALL LIKE ROCK CLIMBING.

HEY, **EARTH BOY!** WHAT'S WITH THE ANCIENT SUIT? YOU FIND THAT IN YOUR GRANDFATHER'S CLOSET?
LOOKS LIKE HE MADE IT HIMSELF OUT OF TINFOIL AND HIS MOM'S DIRTY UNDERWEAR.

DON'T LISTEN TO THEM, BENSON.

LISTEN TO THE **MUSIC**, INSTEAD.

OKAY EVERYONE, LET'S GET TO BOUNCING!

START WITH **LITTLE** JUMPS AT FIRST. JUST **LITTLE** ONES.
bounce
bounce

IT FEELS LIKE I'M FLYING!
YOU'RE **NOT**. JUST BOUNCING. DON'T LOSE FOCUS.
AND DON'T KICK UP SO MUCH **DUST!**

IT'S HARD NOT TO! THE DUST IS SO... SO... EVERYWHERE!
DON'T LAND SO FLAT. PRETEND YOU'RE DIVING, FEET FIRST. LIKE YOU'RE A KNIFE.
YOU NEED TO MINIMIZE DUST OR SORAYA WILL LOSE SIGHT OF YOU, AND THAT MAKES YOU HARDER TO ANCHOR.

DOING OKAY, SORAYA?
NO PROBLEMS! I'M USING MY WINGS TO STABILIZE THE PULL.
IS THAT **CHEATING**?

THIS IS SPACE.
THERE'S NO CHEATING.
ONLY **SURVIVAL**.

BENSON, DON'T OVEREXERT! JUST BECAUSE YOU'RE IN LOW GRAVITY, THAT **DOESN'T** MEAN IT'S NOT STRESSING YOUR BODY.
EASY MOVEMENTS. GRACEFUL. SWIM THROUGH THE AIR.

IT *DOES* FEEL LIKE I'M SWIMMING. OR LIKE I'M FLYING. FOR A LITTLE WHILE, I DON'T CARE ABOUT HOW MY PAPERWORK STILL HASN'T COME THROUGH, OR ABOUT SPRATT AND HIS BULLY FRIENDS, OR ABOUT ANYTHING EXCEPT HOW I'M DANCING IN SPACE, AND THAT SMILE ON SORAYA'S FACE WHENEVER I SEE HER THROUGH THE DUST.

SWITCH!

SORAYA, GO HIGHER THAN BENSON WAS GOING!
LET'S REALLY PUT SOME STRAIN ON HIS MUSCLES!
GIVE HIM A WORKOUT!

WHEE!

EXCELLENT. GOOD WORK!
BUT DON'T FLUTTER YOUR WINGS WHEN YOU'RE CLOSE TO THE SURFACE! IT KICKS UP TOO MUCH DUST!

WHAT'S THE MATTER, LOSER? THAT ANCIENT SUIT OF YOURS CAN'T DEAL WITH THE DUST?
MAYBE YOU SHOULD GIVE IT BACK TO WHATEVER MUSEUM YOU STOLE IT FROM.

FOR ONCE, I'M NOT GOING TO LET SPRATT'S INSULTS BOTHER ME. IT'S EASIER, OUT HERE, TO KNOW THAT HE'S LITERALLY BABBLING NONSENSE INTO AN INFINITE VOID. I DON'T HAVE TO HEAR WHAT HE SAYS; I CAN JUST LET HIS WORDS SLIDE PAST ME AND FADE OFF INTO THE LIMITLESS DISTANCE.

DON'T LET ME GO, BENSON!
I'VE GOT YOU! YOU'RE SAFE!

WHEE! THERE'S SO LITTLE GRAVITY, HERE!
MY WINGS ARE TOO SMALL FOR SUSTAINED FLIGHT, USUALLY, BUT HERE I CAN SOAR! HA HA HA!

SORAYA! WHAT DID I SAY ABOUT FLAPPING YOUR WINGS SO CLOSE TO THE SURFACE!

OH! I'M SORRY!
I GOT TOO EXCITED!

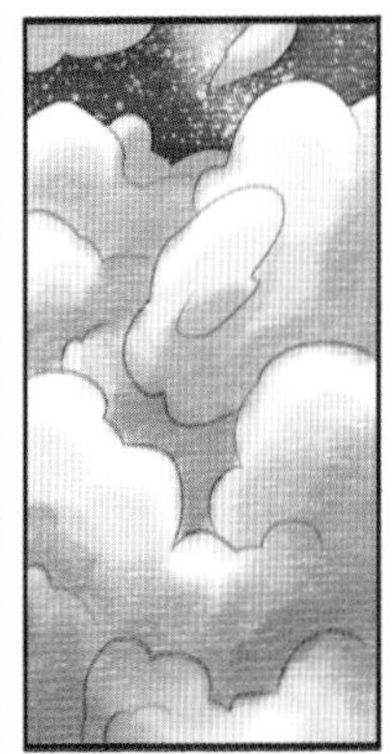

HUH?

WHOA. WHAT'S THAT?

NOT SURE. NEVER SEEN ANYTHING LIKE IT. LET ME GET A SCAN AND...
FVVVV FVVVV

HUH.

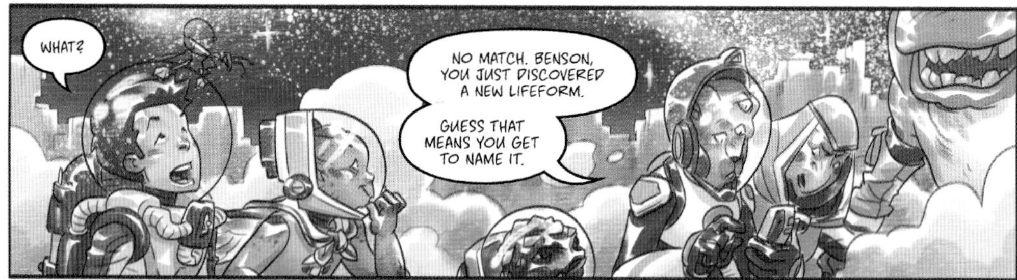
WHAT?
NO MATCH. BENSON, YOU JUST DISCOVERED A NEW LIFEFORM.
GUESS THAT MEANS YOU GET TO NAME IT.

WHAT?
WOW.
WHAT?

I GUESS I'LL CALL IT...A... UH... DUSTY FLATFOOTER.
GOOD ENOUGH, I'LL ENTER ALL THE NECESSARY INFORMATION.
GREAT JOB, BENSON!

THIS FEELS LIKE A DREAM, REALLY. A BIG DUSTY DREAM. AND IT FEELS VINDICATING, TOO, AFTER ALL THE STARES AND THE COUNTLESS INSULTS.

BECAUSE THE ACADEMY TOOK A CHANCE ON ME, AND NOW I'M MAKING MY MARK, MAKING HISTORY, IN THE WAY THAT THEY MUST HAVE BELIEVED I WOULD WHEN THEY GAVE ME THE SCHOLARSHIP. SO, YEAH...
OOO! THERE'S THREE OF THEM, NOW!

FEELS GOOD.

DAY TWENTY-SEVEN: SPACE PIZZA.
AND SO, IN HONOR OF HIS DISCOVERY OF THE FIRST NEW LIFE FORM IN EIGHTY-SEVEN YEARS, BENSON CHOW... FROM HIS HOME PLANET OF JARTH... WILL BE CHOOSING TODAY'S MENU.
THANK YOU, SIR. BUT... IT'S EARTH, NOT JARTH.

WHAT **IS** THIS STUFF?
IT'S CALLED **PIZZA**.
THE SIGNATURE OF ITS ATOMIC VIBRATION IS **BEAUTIFUL**.
IT'S INTERESTING. SMELLS GOOD!

HAVE YOU **SERIOUSLY** NEVER SEEN OR EATEN PIZZA BEFORE? THAT'S LIKE, THE STRANGEST THING I'VE EVER HEARD.
IS IT STILL CALLED PIZZA IF YOU DON'T CUT IT INTO **TRIANGLES**?
I'M PUTTING THIS IN MY SPHERE-GAME. IT COULD BE A QUEST ITEM. OR MAYBE A PLAYABLE CHARACTER? OH, I COULD USE THE CRUST FOR ARMOR!

SO, I'M STARTING TO FIT IN, I THINK. MAYBE? ONLY ABOUT 90% OF THE CADETS LOOK AT ME LIKE I'M A FREAK, NOW, SO... THAT'S PROGRESS! AND IT'S *MIND-BENDING* TO REALIZE THAT, FOR MY DISCOVERY, I'LL BE IN THE *OFFICIAL* HISTORY OF THE KAYRUS ACADEMY.

I MEAN, SURE, FINDING A DUSTY FLATFOOTER ISN'T AS AWESOME AS THE BROKEN BROTHERS OF THE FOG FINDING THAT ENTIRE GALAXY OF LIVING PLANETS, BUT IT STILL FEELS PRETTY GOOD.

IT'S A START.

"MY FAMILY MADE OUR FORTUNE AS WARSUIT DESIGNERS. WE STILL DO A BIT OF WORK IN THOSE AREAS, BUT MOSTLY WE'VE MOVED INTO...

OUR PEOPLE COME FROM **INSECTS**.
WE USED TO BE **THIIIIIIS** SMALL.

"OUR PLANET IS **CHKLITN**. DON'T TRY TO PRONOUNCE IT RIGHT. YOU'D NEED TWO TONGUES. MOST LIFE ON CHKLITN HAS WINGS. OURSELVES INCLUDED, OF COURSE. OUR WINGS WORK MUCH BETTER THERE, BECAUSE IT'S LARGELY GASEOUS. THE ATMOSPHERE IS PERFECT FOR FLIGHT.

"I CAN SEE THROUGH MIST, FOG, ANYTHING LIKE THAT. MY PEOPLE HAVE WHAT YOU WOULD CALL AN INNATE RADAR, BUT MORE ADVANCED. WE SEE VIBRATIONS. ANY MOVEMENT AT ALL."

AND OUR NOSES "SEE" IN THREE DIMENSIONS, TOO. EVOLVING ON A MIST PLANET WILL TAKE CARE OF THAT.
I MISS THE SCENTS ON CHKLITN. MOST WORLDS SMELL BARREN TO ME. I MISS SMELLING CINNAMON MISTS AND FIRE-TINGED FOGS.

"CHKLITNIANS ARE KNOWN AS SOME OF THE FEDERATION'S BEST NAVIGATORS. WE SEE THE UNIVERSE DIFFERENTLY THAN ANYONE ELSE. NAVIGATION IS MUSIC. IT'S ALL ABOUT THE CHORDS THE PLANETS ARE PLAYING, THE NOTES THAT LIGHT PLAYS WHEN IT SPEEDS ALONG ITS PATHWAYS. THE SHRILL HISS OF A NEUTRINO SLIDING THROUGH ATOMIC STRUCTURES. IT'S A SYMPHONY."

I'LL JUST SIT HERE AND BE JEALOUS, THEN. WISH I COULD HEAR THAT MUSIC, OR THAT I HAD WINGS AND COULD FLY LIKE YOU.
DON'T BE JEALOUS. WE ALL HAVE OUR OWN WINGS AND OUR OWN MUSIC. YOU'LL FIND YOURS.

DAY SIXTY-EIGHT: THIS IS INCREDIBLE. I NEVER THOUGHT I'D DO SOMETHING LIKE THIS.

I'M ON THE PLANET *LISS*, IN THE MIDDLE OF THE REMOTE DOPPELGÄNGER NEBULA, AND I'M TEACHING THE NATIVES HOW TO MAKE FIRE.

ONE OF THEM IS SKETCHING A DRAWING OF ME ON A ROCK. I'M DESTINED TO BE IN THEIR MYTHOLOGY.

PRINN, MY ADVISOR AND THE EARTH STUDIES PROFESSOR, CAME ALONG TO OBSERVE. NOT ABSOLUTELY SURE IF SHE'S OBSERVING THE LISSIANS, OR *ME*.
WE NORMALLY DON'T INTERFERE IN PRIMITIVE SOCIETIES, BENSON, BUT THIS IS A SPECIAL CASE.

THAT'S SX-563-KR, UP THERE IN THE SKY, AND BY ALL OUR ESTIMATIONS IT WILL GO SUPERNOVA BEFORE THE LISSIANS DEVELOP SPACE TRAVEL.
MEANING THAT IF WE DON'T SPEED THEM UP A BIT, THEY ALL DIE HERE.

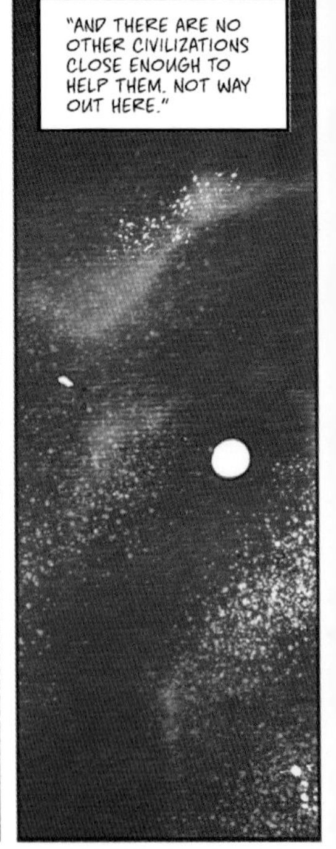
"AND THERE ARE NO OTHER CIVILIZATIONS CLOSE ENOUGH TO HELP THEM. NOT WAY OUT HERE."

"WAY OUT HERE" IS RIGHT. SINCE OUR FLENNITE USE IS RESTRICTED, WE HAD TO GO INTO SUSPENDED ANIMATION TO MAKE IT HERE TO LISS.

IT TOOK ALMOST THIRTY DAYS. AN ENTIRE MONTH... VANISHED. HOW STRANGE. HOW LONG HAVE BOGLEY AND I BEEN FRIENDS, THEN? TWO MONTHS, OR THREE MONTHS? DOES TIME EVEN COUNT IF WE WERE FROZEN?

DAYS ARE WEIRD AT KAYRUS ANYWAY. DAYS ARE SO STRANGE IN SPACE. I DON'T MEAN THAT THE DAYS ARE LONGER OR SHORTER DEPENDING ON VARIOUS SOLAR ROTATIONS, I MEAN THAT TIME ITSELF PASSES FASTER OR SLOWER IN DIFFERENT PARTS OF THE UNIVERSE, RELATIVE TO OTHER PARTS.

TWO MINUTES IN ONE PLACE COULD TAKE TWO *YEARS* IN ANOTHER. IT'S SO BIZARRE. I GUESS THAT'S PART OF GETTING OLDER, JOINING THE REST OF THE UNIVERSE, UNDERSTANDING OTHER CIVILIZATIONS. THERE ARE SO MANY PERSPECTIVES, OUT HERE. IT'S SO EASY TO GET LOST.

PRINN SAYS THAT I CAN EITHER STAND OBSTINATELY IN THE CURRENT AND LET IT FLOW AROUND ME, PRETENDING IT DOESN'T MATTER, OR I CAN DIVE RIGHT IN AND SWIM. I ASKED HER, WHAT ABOUT BUILDING A BOAT? I MEANT IT AS A *JOKE*.

SHE SAID, "DON'T DO THAT. IT'S TOO LONELY. YOU HAVE TO BE PART OF LIFE. PART OF THE WATER."

DAY NINETY-THREE: PEOPLE SUCK.

SO, I PUT YOU IN THE GAME. YOU'RE A BLACK HOLE PILOT. SEE, THERE YOU ARE.
THIS IS JUST PRE-IMMERSION MODELING, OF COURSE. I'LL DEVELOP THE DEEP-SPHERE IMMERSION AS SOON AS--

PFAFF!
URGG!

WHAT THE HECK IS **THIS**?
HA HA HA HA HA! YES!
HA HA HA HA HA!

OH NO.

YOU PUT A DUSTY FLATFOOTER IN MY FOOD?
OF COURSE! YOU **LOVE** THEM SO MUCH, I FIGURED YOU'D WANT TO **EAT** ONE.

ONLY **THREE** OF THESE KNOWN IN THE WHOLE UNIVERSE, AND YOU JUST **KILLED** ONE TO MAKE A **JOKE**? THAT'S NOT HUMAN.
OF COURSE IT'S NOT!
BEING **HUMAN** WOULD MAKE ME **SICK**.

DAY NINETY-SIX: TODAY WAS THE WORST DAY OF MY LIFE.
DIRECTOR SQUA-TRONT

SO, YOU'RE CHECKING TO SEE IF YOUR PAPERWORK IS APPROVED YET? IS THAT RIGHT, BRESSON?
THAT'S RIGHT, SIR. AND IT'S BENSON.
YES. YES. OF COURSE.

LET'S SEE WHAT THE FILES SAY. I DON'T REMEMBER ALL YOUR ADMISSION DETAILS RIGHT OFF HAND, BUT WE'LL TAKE A LOOK AT ALL YOUR INFORMATION.
PROFESSOR SQUA-TRONT, YOU HAVE A CALL FROM YOUR WIFE. SHE SAYS THE YOUNGEST EGG IN YOUR NEST IS ON FIRE.

WHAT? OH NO! THAT'S **HORRIBLE**!
HUH? NO. THAT'S GOOD. **VERY** GOOD!

BUT I SHOULD TAKE THIS CALL. I'LL BE RIGHT BACK.

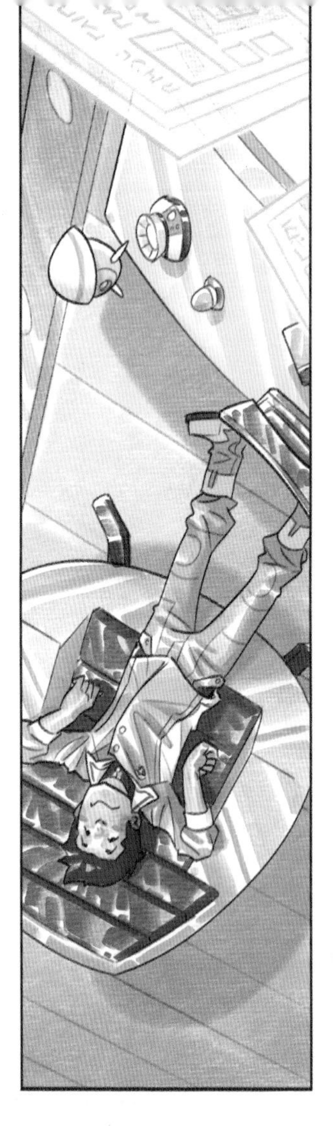

CADET BENSON CHOW: I AM REGISTERING THAT YOU ARE BORED AND NERVOUS. MAY I BE OF ASSISTANCE? WOULD YOU LIKE TO PLAY A GAME?
I HAVE A SELECTION OF OVER THIRTY-SEVEN THOUSAND GAMES OF--

ACTUALLY, COULD I LOOK AT MY FILE? I WANT TO SEE WHAT'S GOING ON.
NORMALLY I WOULD REFUSE SUCH A REQUEST, BUT AS THE DIRECTOR HAS LEFT YOUR FILE **OPEN**, I CAN CONSTRUE THAT AS **PERMISSION** ON HIS PART.
WHAT WOULD YOU LIKE TO SEE IN YOUR FILE, CADET BENSON CHOW OF THE PLANET EARTH?

WELL, THE STATUS OF MY ADMISSION PAPERS, I GUESS?
ADMISSION PAPERS ARE PENDING. CURRENTLY LACKING THREE OF THE FOUR NECESSARY SIGNATURES.

OH. DANG. OKAY.
YOU KNOW, I'M ALSO WONDERING... WHY DID THE ACADEMY CHOOSE ME? I MEAN, OF ALL THE AVAILABLE CANDIDATES, WHY DID I GET THE SCHOLARSHIP?

IT'S MY TEST SCORES, RIGHT? MY BRAIN SCAN? MY EMPATHY IMPRINT?
I'M CURIOUS WHY I WAS CHOSEN TO BE THE FIRST EVER CADET FROM EARTH.
IS IT BECAUSE I HAVE A WAY WITH ANIMALS, LIKE, ON MY FARM, OR MY VOLUNTEER WORK AT THE GRAND CANYON CITY ZOO THE PAST COUPLE WINTERS?

NEGATIVE. ACCORDING TO THE DIRECTOR NOTES IN YOUR FILES, EARTH IS RATED AS AN UNPOPULAR PLANET WITH STRANGE-LOOKING INHABITANTS.
NORMALLY, THE HISTORIC KAYRUS ACADEMY WOULD NOT HAVE ADMITTED YOU OR ANY EARTHLING UNDER ANY CIRCUMSTANCES.

UNFORTUNATELY, FOR THE PAST FEW CENTURIES, FUNDING HAS DECLINED AT KAYRUS, MEANING THAT BUDGETARY CONCERNS NOW TAKE PRECEDENCE OVER THE UNFORTUNATE ADMISSION OF UNDESIRABLES.

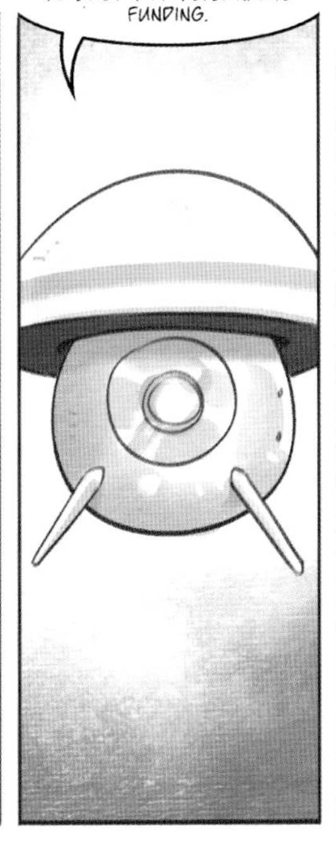
THE KAYRUS ACADEMY FORTUNES WERE ONCE BASED ON FLENNITE AND TRIBIUM, BUT RESOURCES HAVE DRIED UP, FORCING THE ACADEMY TO LOOK FOR ALTERNATIVE FUNDING.

AS IT HAPPENS, THE GALACTIC FEDERATION OFFERS FUNDING TO ALL SCHOOLS THAT MEET MINIMUM MINORITY STANDARDS.
I HAVE HERE A NOTE MENTIONING EARTH AS A POSSIBLE WAY TO FILL THIS QUOTA REQUIREMENT.

ACCORDING TO THE DIRECTOR'S NOTES IN YOUR FILE, YOU ARE, I QUOTE, "NO MORE THAN A BUDGETARY CHECKMARK."

YOUR NAME WAS CHOSEN FROM A RANDOM LOTTERY OF AVAILABLE EARTH STUDENTS.

UNDER THE HEADING FOR ADMISSION RECOMMENDATIONS, DIRECTOR SQUA-TRONT HAS ADDED THE FOLLOWING STATEMENT:
"THE PROPOSED CADET IS NO ONE SPECIAL, WITH NO OUTSTANDING QUALITIES, BUT AS HIS ENROLLMENT WILL ADD 1.7 MILLION GALACTIC CREDITS TO SCHOOL FUNDING, ADMISSION IS RECOMMENDED."

SEVERAL TEACHERS, UPON HEARING AN EARTHLING WOULD BE ADMITTED, RESIGNED THEIR POSTS. THE ACADEMY CONSIDERED THIS A BONUS, REMOVING THEIR SALARIES FROM THE BUDGET AND--
SHUT UP!!!

JUST... SHUT UP!

WHAT'S YOUR PROBLEM NOW, TRASHLING?
SHUT UP!

LET'S GET TO **RUNNING**! **TEN** MILES THIS MORNING! LET'S SEE SOME **FIRE**! LET'S SEE SOME **SPIRIT**!

NAVIGATION IS MATH. OR MUSIC. OR INSTINCT. YOU NEED THEM ALL.

A CADET NEEDS FAMILIARITY WITH GALACTIC LAW.

BENSON. WANNA DO SOMETHING TONIGHT? WE COULD JUST HANG OUT WITH LORNA AND SORAYA. THEY SAID WE COULD COME OVER.
WANNA DO SOMETHING? BENSON? HEY! HELLOOOOO?

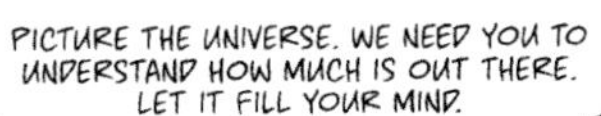
PICTURE THE UNIVERSE. WE NEED YOU TO UNDERSTAND HOW MUCH IS OUT THERE. LET IT FILL YOUR MIND.

THE DARKNESS IS OUT THERE. IT NEVER ENDS.
SWIM, PUNKS, **SWIM**! YOU THINK WE'RE HERE FOR **GAMES**? LET'S **GO**! LET'S SEE SOME **FIRE**!

IN EMERGENCY SITUATIONS, YOU MIGHT HAVE TO GEAR UP, **QUICK**!
LET'S SEE YOU SET SOME **RECORDS** FOR GETTING INTO YOUR SUITS! READY ON **THREE**!

I BROUGHT **PIZZA**. IT WAS IN SQUARES BUT I CUT IT INTO TRIANGLES. NOW IT'S REAL PIZZA.
WOULD YOU LIKE TO GO FOR A PICNIC? A WALK OR SOMETHING? BENSON?
COME ON, TALK TO ME.

STRATEGY IS YOUR KEY. BE OPEN-MINDED. YOU'LL NEVER BE BIGGER THAN THE UNIVERSE, AND IT **IS** OUT TO GET YOU, SO ALL YOU CAN DO IS STAY SHARP, AND KEEP YOUR FOCUS...
...OR YOU GET CHEWED UP AND SPIT OUT.

HEY, BENSON! I HEARD THE NEWS. TOUGH BREAK!

I MEAN, WHEN I SAW YOU LEAVING THE OFFICE THE OTHER DAY, I WONDERED WHAT GOT YOU SO DEPRESSED...
... SO I WENT AND TOOK A LOOK, AND I FOUND THAT INFO ON THE COMPUTER, JUST ALL OUT THERE FOR ANYONE TO SEE.

YOU KNOW, ALL THAT STUFF ABOUT YOU ONLY BEING A QUOTA STUDENT?
ALL THAT STUFF ABOUT HOW THE SCHOOL DOESN'T REALLY WANT YOU HERE?

ALL THAT STUFF ABOUT HOW YOU DON'T BELONG HERE.
THAT EARTH IS A PRIMITIVE PLANET. THAT YOUR FRIENDS ARE COMPLETE LOSERS, TOO.
THAT YOU STILL POOP THE BED AT NIGHT, AND THAT YOU HIDE IN BATHROOMS, STARING IN MIRRORS, CRYING TO YOURSELF, WISHING YOU WEREN'T SO UGLY.

BUT DON'T WORRY... I'M HERE FOR YOU.
I KNOW IT SUCKS TO BE ALONE, SO I COPIED EVERYTHING I FOUND ON THE COMPUTER, AND I SENT IT AROUND TO EVERYONE IN SCHOOL, SO NOW, WE ALL KNOW EVERYTHING ABOUT YOU.
ISN'T THAT NICE OF ME? YOU AREN'T ALONE ANYMORE, EARTH SCUM.

BECAUSE EVERYONE KNOWS.
ha ha ha ha
ha ha

DAY ONE HUNDRED AND THREE: NOTHINGNESS.

HAVE YOU EVER **SMELLED** AN EARTH PERSON? I WOULDN'T ADVISE IT.

HIS VOICE IRRITATES ME.

WHY'S HE EVEN HERE? SOMEBODY SHOULD **DO** SOMETHING.

I HAVE A CLASS WITH HIM. I MAKE SURE TO SIT ACROSS THE ROOM.

MAYBE THE SCHOOL IS TESTING US? SOME SORT OF PRIMITIVE STUDIES PROGRAM?

HE LOOKS LIKE A PET, DOESN'T HE? HE DEFINITELY LOOKS LIKE A PET. I'M SURE EARTH CHILDREN ARE FURRY AND ADORABLE.

ALL THEY KNOW IS KILLING. THERE'S NO CULTURE ON EARTH. IT'S JUST ROCKS AND BLOOD.

HOW MANY EARTHERS DOES IT TAKE TO CHANGE A LIGHT BULB?

IF YOU WIGGLE A **LEASH** AT AN EARTHER, THEY FALL ON THEIR BACKS AND **PEE**.

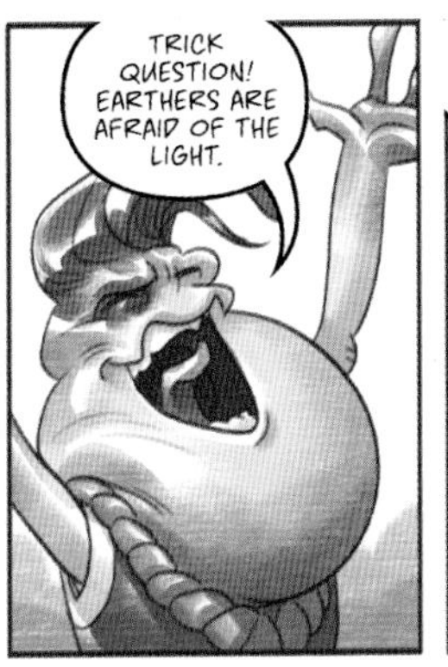
TRICK QUESTION! EARTHERS ARE AFRAID OF THE LIGHT.

SHOULDN'T THIS CHAIR BE DISINFECTED? THAT GROSS BOY WAS SITTING HERE.

THEY SHOULD ALL BE ENSLAVED.

LOOK, I DREW A PICTURE OF EARTH! HA HA HA HA!

UGGH. I'M SURPRISED IT CAN EVEN **TALK**.

THEY EAT THEIR YOUNG.
I HEARD IT. IT'S **TRUE**.

DAY ONE HUNDRED AND FOUR: SURVIVAL, I GUESS.

PROFESSOR LURRIG, MAY I BE EXCUSED? THE EARTH BOY IS MAKING ME SICK.

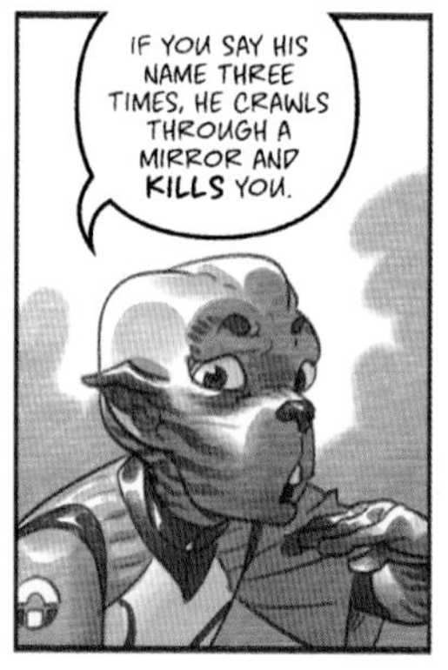
IF YOU SAY HIS NAME THREE TIMES, HE CRAWLS THROUGH A MIRROR AND **KILLS** YOU.

ON EARTH, THEY BUILD THEIR HOUSES OUT OF DUNG.

I DON'T KNOW WHAT TO DO. HE BARELY TALKS ANYMORE.

HEY, BENSON! FETCH! BENSON! **FETCH**!

IF YOU DO SOMETHING WRONG IN CLASS, THEY MAKE YOU SIT NEXT TO THAT EARTH KID.

NO WONDER HE DISCOVERED AN INSECT. HE MUST BE **CRAWLING** WITH THEM.

I DREAMED HE **BIT** ME. IT WAS TERRIFYING.

PUPPET SHOW! **PUPPET SHOW**!

HE SHOULDN'T BE IN THE **ACADEMY**. HE SHOULD BE IN THE **ZOO**.

I WIN TEN CREDITS IF I TOUCH THAT EARTHER, BUT WHAT IF HE BITES MY FINGERS OFF?

PARTY! **PARTY**! WE FOUND SOME OF YOUR EARTH DRINK. IT'S MADE FROM GRAPES AND IT'S CALLED **LEMONADE**.

I HEARD HE BIT A GIRL. APPARENTLY SHE **DIED**.

SO, APPARENTLY, LEMONADE IS MADE FROM **LEMONS**, AND WHAT **WE** DRANK IS CALLED **WINE**, AND IT'S ALCOHOLIC, AND LORNA FLEW AROUND AND PUKED ON OUR CEILING.

I WONDER IF HE CAN BE TAUGHT TO DO TRICKS? IS HE SMART ENOUGH?

DAY ONE HUNDRED AND SIX: THE END.
ENOUGH!
INTERVENTION TIME, ROOMIE.

IT'S "FORGET EVERYTHING ELSE" NIGHT. WE'RE GOING TO PLAY GAMES.
I MADE YOU PIZZA. IT CAUGHT ON FIRE. YOU WILL STILL EAT IT.
UH, OKAY.

THIS IS STILL PRE-IMMERSION MODELING, BUT WE CAN PLAY SOME OF IT. AND... THERE'S THE CHARACTER I BASED ON YOU.
SEE? IT'S NOT REALLY DANGEROUS. IT JUST MOPES AROUND. MUTTERING TO ITSELF. SHUFFLING ITS FEET. SIGHING ALL THE TIME.
I GET IT! I GET IT!

THERE. YOUR NOSE IS ENTIRELY COVERED. NOW LET'S SEE IF YOU CAN STILL TELL... WHICH ONE IS SORAYA?
UHH. RIGHT THERE.
WOW! THAT'S AMAZING!

DAY ONE HUNDRED AND SEVEN: FAMILY.
SORRY I HAVEN'T CALLED IN A WHILE, SIS. IT'S BEEN... ROUGH. THE PRESSURE HAS BEEN REALLY WORKING ON ME.
I GET THAT. LET ME TELL YOU SOMETHING, THOUGH.

WHENEVER THE PRESSURE IS TOO MUCH FOR ME, I THINK OF SWIMMING. IT MAKES THINGS EASIER TO DEAL WITH.
PRESSURE IS EASY WHEN YOU'RE SWIMMING. IT'S THE EASIEST EQUATION IN THE UNIVERSE.
ALL YOU NEED TO DO IS KEEP IN MIND THAT THE MOMENT YOU STOP SWIMMING... YOU SINK.

DAY ONE HUNDRED AND TEN: A NIGHT OUT!
SHIVER SHARK! Private Investigator
FULL IMMERSION-SPHERE ENTERTAINMENT!

I LOVE ALL THE MOVIES IN THE **SHIVER SHARK** SERIES. HAVE YOU SEEN **SHIVER SHARK: BRIDE OF THE VOLCANO**?
OOO. YEAH! THAT'S THE ONE WITH THE GIRL WITH VOLCANIC FINGERS. I ACTUALLY BOUGHT THE LAVA GLOVES FOR LAST HALLOWEEN.

IT'S NICE TO SEE YOU OUT OF YOUR ROOM.
YEAH. I GUESS I CAN'T FEEL SORRY FOR MYSELF FOREVER.

WELL, YOU **TRIED**, AND THAT'S IMPORTANT.
HEY! YOU TWO! OVER **HERE**!

SHIVER SHARK IS FIGHTING THE **LUPUS MOB**!
PUNCH!

OH CRAP! VOLCANO BRIDE IS **BACK**!

DAY ONE HUNDRED AND TWELVE: PRINN HAS BEEN CHECKING IN ON ME, LATELY. HONESTLY, SHE'S BEEN MORE OF A THERAPIST THAN AN ADVISOR. MAYBE THE LINE BETWEEN THE TWO IS THIN. EITHER WAY, SHE'S NICE TO TALK TO. PLUS, SHE'S THE ONLY ONE WHO CAN GET ME PEANUT BUTTER CUPS.

DOES LIFE GET ANY EASIER WHEN YOU GET OLDER?
WELL, I SUPPOSE IT'S TRUE THAT FOR SOME PEOPLE, IT GETS EASIER TO DEAL WITH BAD THINGS. AND WITH OTHER PEOPLE, WELL... YOU GROW A THICKER SKIN.

LITERALLY, IN SOME CASES.

I JUST DON'T UNDERSTAND HOW SOME PEOPLE WORK. I MEAN, SPRATT, WHAT'S HE GET OUT OF BEING A BULLY?
HE'S **AFRAID**, REALLY. MOST BULLIES ARE. SO, BY BELITTLING YOU, HE GETS TO FEEL BETTER ABOUT HIMSELF.
BULLYING IS THE DEFENSE MECHANISM OF THE WEAK.

YOU KNOW, MAYBE **THIS** IS WEAK, BUT SOMETIMES WHEN IT'S BAD, I JUST WANT TO JUMP IN A ROCKET AND SOAR AWAY TO A DISTANT GALAXY.
YEAH, WELL, WITH THE **FLENNITE SHORTAGE**, MAYBE YOU BETTER STICK CLOSER TO HOME.

ANYWAY, I THINK THERE'S A **CERTAIN SOMEONE** WHO WOULD MISS YOU.
BOGLEY? HE'D FIND ANOTHER ROOMMATE.

ACKK? WHAT ARE YOU DOING?
STUDYING YOUR CRANIUM.
THE HEART OF A DARK STAR IS CONSIDERED THE DENSEST MATERIAL IN THE UNIVERSE, BUT IT SEEMS YOUR HEAD IS EVEN MORE DENSE.

GROSS. LOOK AT **THAT**.
DOWN IN THE MUCK AND THE MIRE AGAIN, EH PRINN?
BUG OFF, SCHEBBLEHORN!

WHAT WAS **THAT** ABOUT?
THE OTHER TEACHERS THINK I'M WEIRD FOR TALKING WITH YOU. I FIND THEIR REACTIONS AMUSING, TO BE HONEST.
THEY'RE SUPPOSED TO HAVE OPEN MINDS, BUT THEY'RE LIKE ADULT VERSIONS OF SPRATT.

YEAH, WELL SEE, THAT'S MY PROBLEM. I'M **DOOMED** HERE AT KAYRUS, AREN'T I?
I MEAN, **NOBODY** WANTS ME HERE. I'M ONLY A QUOTA STUDENT. IF IT WASN'T FOR THE FUNDING, THERE'S NO **WAY** I'D BE HERE.

HMM, I SUPPOSE THAT'S ONE WAY OF--
OH. WAIT. I WAS THINKING ABOUT GOING UP THAT STAIRCASE, BUT...
BUT WHAT?
WELL, I MEAN, **BEFORE** WE CAN GO UP THE STAIRS, WE **OBVIOUSLY** HAVE TO DETERMINE WHO **BUILT** THE STAIRWAY, AND **WHY** THEY BUILT THE STAIRWAY.
WE HAVE TO KNOW WHAT THE STAIRCASE **MEANS** ON A DEEPER LEVEL.
AFTER ALL, IT'S NOT LIKE WE CAN JUST **USE** A STAIRCASE SIMPLY BECAUSE THE **OPPORTUNITY** IS THERE TO USE ONE.

IS THIS SOME SORT OF MORAL ANALOGY?

ONLY IF YOU WERE PAYING ATTENTION.

DAY ONE HUNDRED AND FOURTEEN: SWEAT.
THREE HUNDRED PUSHUPS, NOW!

THOSE WITH EXTRA ARMS, YOU CAN ONLY USE TWO!
THOSE WITH WINGS, I BETTER NOT SEE THEM SO MUCH AS FLUTTER!

THIS IS ABOUT GUTTING IT OUT! THIS IS ABOUT REACHING DEEP!
ANYBODY WHO CAN'T GIVE ME THREE HUNDRED PUSHUPS HAS TO RING THIS BELL AND LET EVERYONE KNOW THAT YOU CAN'T TAKE IT!

HOW ABOUT YOU, BENSON CHOW? YOU LOOK LIKE THE WEAKEST AND MOST PATHETIC CREATURE I'VE EVER SEEN!
MIGHT AS WELL SAVE TIME AND RING THAT BELL RIGHT NOW! I'VE HEARD ALL ABOUT PEOPLE FROM EARTH!

I HEAR IT'S A CRYBABY PLANET!
I HEAR YOU WEAR DIAPERS FROM CRADLE TO GRAVE!
I HEARD THAT YOUR GUTTURAL EARTH LANGUAGE HAS TWO HUNDRED DIFFERENT WORDS THAT MEAN, "I CAN'T DO IT!"

AND FIVE HUNDRED WORDS FOR "I GIVE UP."

"I WAS YOUNG, THEN. BARELY THREE HUNDRED. THE CLASSES WERE WILDLY POPULAR IN THOSE DAYS. ANYTHING **NEW** INTERESTS PEOPLE. WISH WE COULD HAVE KEPT UP THAT INITIAL ENTHUSIASM."

DAY ONE HUNDRED AND FIFTEEN: SPACE JUMP.
HOW YA DOING, BENSON?

MY ARMS ACHE LIKE CRAZY. DID FOUR HUNDRED PUSHUPS TODAY. IN A ROW.
YOU ONLY **HAD** TO DO **THREE** HUNDRED.

YEAH.
I KNOW.

I'M GLAD YOU'RE HERE, BENSON. I'M GLAD YOU'RE MY FRIEND.
SAME HERE, BOGLEY.
YOU GUYS! SUIT UP! JUMP INTO SPACE WITH US! IT'S LIKE... **INFINITE** OUT HERE!

DAY ONE HUNDRED AND FIFTEEN: PHILOSOPHY, I GUESS?
SO, HOW DO I GET SPRATT TO LAY OFF? IS THERE SOME WAY I CAN REACH HIM? SHOULD I EVEN TRY TO BE FRIENDS?
THERE'S NO EASY ANSWER BEYOND, YES... YOU SHOULD TRY. BUT SORRY, IT PROBABLY WON'T WORK.

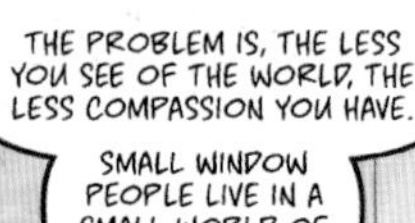

WHY NOT?
LET ME PUT IT THIS WAY... LOOK OUT THAT WINDOW.

OKAY?
EXCELLENT.
SEE THAT VAST WORLD OUT THERE? THAT'S WHAT MOST PEOPLE SEE.

BUT SOME PEOPLE SEE A SMALLER WORLD.
THEIR CLOSED MINDS ONLY GIVE THEM SO MUCH WINDOW TO LOOK THROUGH.
VRRRRR

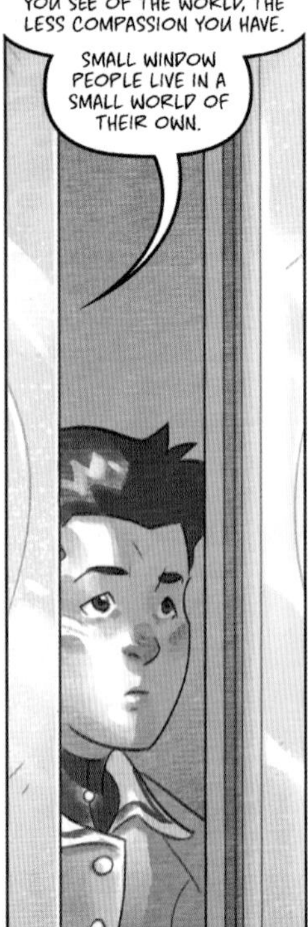
THE PROBLEM IS, THE LESS YOU SEE OF THE WORLD, THE LESS COMPASSION YOU HAVE.
SMALL WINDOW PEOPLE LIVE IN A SMALL WORLD OF THEIR OWN.

WORSE, PEOPLE LIKE SPRATT DON'T EVEN HAVE WINDOWS. IT'S JUST MIRRORS.
THEY ONLY WANT TO SEE THEMSELVES. ANYTHING ELSE MAKES THEM ANGRY.

THE TRICK IN LIFE IS TO KEEP YOUR OWN WINDOW OPEN.
NEVER MAKE THE MISTAKE OF THINKING ANY TWO PEOPLE ARE ALIKE, JUST BECAUSE THEY'RE FROM THE SAME PLANET OR WEAR THE SAME UNIFORM.
EVERYONE IS DIFFERENT. GIVE EVERYONE A CHANCE.

THE UNIVERSE IS VAST AND THERE ARE SO MANY GOOD PEOPLE, FROM ALL PLANETS, ALL CULTURES, PEOPLE WHO WILL ALWAYS HAVE YOUR BACK.
STEP OUTSIDE THE WINDOWS, AND YOU CAN MAKE YOURSELF A REAL LIFE.

DAY ONE HUNDRED AND SIXTEEN: SORAYA.
PAIR UP! TODAY WE'RE ON CLOSE COMBAT SKILLS! HAND TO HAND! TENTACLE TO PAW! PAIR UP! FIND YOURSELF A SPARRING PARTNER!

SO I SAW THAT BENSON IDIOT THE OTHER DAY. WHAT'S HE EVEN DOING HERE? IN A CADET UNIFORM? THE ONLY THING HE SHOULD BE DOING IS CLEANING UP AFTER US. LIKE, DOING THE BATHROOMS.
RIGHT? THAT'S ALL SOMEONE FROM EARTH IS WORTH. WHAT REALLY GETS ME IS THAT HE SEEMS TO THINK HE ACTUALLY BELONGS HERE. WISH HE'D HURRY UP AND FLUNK OUT.

HE SEEMS TO THINK HE'S SPECIAL.

WHAT ARE YOU LOOKING AT?
HEY... I KNOW HER. THAT'S THE GIRL THAT HANGS OUT WITH--

TWO THINGS YOU SHOULD KNOW.
THE FIRST IS... BENSON IS SPECIAL.
AND THE SECOND IS...

... I JUST CHOSE YOU FOR MY SPARRING PARTNER.

POW!!
GUHH!

DAY ONE HUNDRED AND SEVENTEEN: THE ART OF BEING SPECIAL.
SO LET ME ASK YOU, WHAT **IS** SPECIAL?

EVERYONE HERE IS STRUGGLING TO BE NOTICED, TO BE SPECIAL, BUT SOME PEOPLE ARE DOING IT IN DIFFERENT WAYS.
YOU'RE DOING IT BY STUDYING HARD, LEARNING EVERYTHING YOU CAN, TRYING TO ACHIEVE THE KAYRUS RANGER IDEALS.

"OTHER PEOPLE ARE TRYING TO BECOME SPECIAL BY BEING THE FUNNIEST, OR BY HAVING THE MOST FRIENDS, OR IN THE CASE OF SOMEONE LIKE SPRATT, BY PRETENDING THEY'RE ALREADY SPECIAL, ON ACCOUNT OF THEIR FAMILIES. STUCKERS'S FATHER IS THE HEAD OF CTHONNI ENTERPRISES, MAKING HIM ONE OF THE RICHEST MEN IN THE TRIGALAXY AREA. THE MAN OWNS WHOLE SOLAR SYSTEMS."

BUT LET ME ASK YOU, DOES IT GET SOMEONE BETTER **TEST** SCORES JUST BECAUSE THEIR **FAMILIES** ARE RICH AND POWERFUL?
NO. IT DOESN'T.

TRICK QUESTION, BENSON.
IT DOES.

MOST TEACHERS WOULD GIVE A FAR BETTER GRADE TO SPRATT THAN THEY WOULD TO YOU, EVEN IF YOUR ANSWERS WERE IDENTICAL.
BECAUSE PEOPLE SEE WHAT THEY **EXPECT** TO SEE, AND WHAT THEY **WANT** TO SEE.

EVERYONE IS BIASED. THAT'S JUST THE WAY LIFE IS. YOU'LL HAVE TO WORK TWICE AS HARD TO GET THE SAME RESULTS. EVERY STEP YOU TAKE NEEDS TO BE FASTER, BETTER.
AND WOULD YOU LIKE TO KNOW WHAT MAKES IT FAIR?
UH. SURE?

NOTHING DOES. NOTHING MAKES IT FAIR.
THERE'S NO RULE THAT SAYS THINGS HAVE TO BE FAIR, AND NO ONE TO ENFORCE THE RULE IF THERE WAS ONE.

IT COULD TAKE CENTURIES BEFORE CERTAIN PARTS OF THE GALACTIC FEDERATION THINK EARTH HAS ANY VALUE. IT MIGHT NEVER HAPPEN.
PEOPLE HAVE BIASES INGRAINED INTO THEIR SYSTEMS.

HERE, LOOK AT THIS.
WHOA! WHAT'S THAT?

THAT'S A STRAAIAN.
HUH? LIKE BOGLEY?
IS THERE, LIKE, A LOT OF DIFFERENCE BETWEEN THE WAY STRAAIANS LOOK?

NO. THAT'S JUST THE WAY PEOPLE USED TO THINK THEY LOOKED.
WHEN THEY FIRST JOINED THE FEDERATION, THE STRAAIANS WERE ALWAYS PORTRAYED AS THE BAD GUYS IN SPHERE-MOVIES, AND THEY ALWAYS LOOKED INCREDIBLY SAVAGE.
IT LASTED FOR CENTURIES IN ALL FORMS OF POPULAR ENTERTAINMENT.

BUT, ANYONE WHO'S EVER MET A STRAAIAN WOULD KNOW BETTER!
DOESN'T MATTER. THERE'S A DIFFERENCE BETWEEN HOW AN **INDIVIDUAL** LOOKS AT SOMEONE, VERSUS HOW A **SOCIETY** SEES THEM.

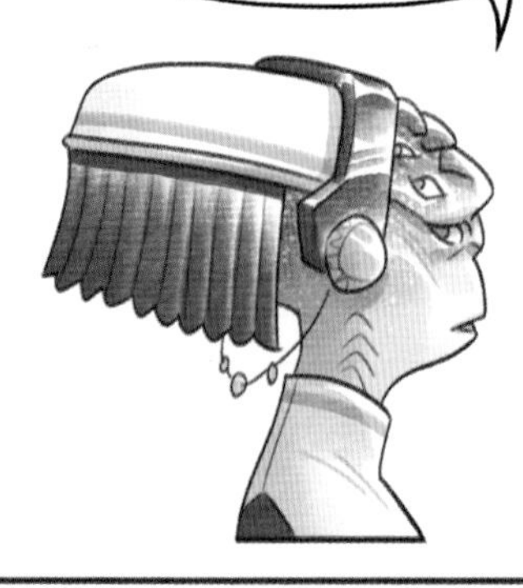
LIKE YOU SAY, ANYONE WHO MEETS A STRAAIAN **KNOWS** THEY'RE DIFFERENT THAN SEEN IN THE SPHERES, BUT...

"...ENTERTAINMENT AND MEDIA HAVE DRILLED CERTAIN BIASES INTO THEIR SUBCONSCIOUS.

"AFTER SEEING A CULTURE PORTRAYED AS SAVAGE VILLAINS FOR A FEW HUNDRED YEARS, IT BECOMES TRUTH FROM A **SOCIETY'S** VIEWPOINT, NO MATTER WHAT THE ACTUAL EVIDENCE TELLS THEM, OR HOW ANY ONE **INDIVIDUAL** FEELS.

SO YES... IT'S GOING TO TAKE TIME BEFORE GALACTIC SOCIETY WARMS UP TO PEOPLE FROM EARTH.
IS IT **FRUSTRATING**? YES.
AND IS IT **RIGHT**? NO.

BUT PROGRESS **IS** BEING MADE. IT JUST TAKES GENERATIONS.
HONESTLY, IF YOU'D SHOWED UP TWO CENTURIES AGO, EVERYONE WOULD HAVE WONDERED WHERE YOUR POISON TUSKS WERE AT.

INSTEAD OF JUST A SORRY FEW.

DAY ONE HUNDRED AND TWENTY: SOMETIMES IT HELPS TO HAVE A WALK ALONE. WORK MY THOUGHTS OUT. THERE'S AN UNUSED SECTION OF PORT. SHUT DOWN SINCE THE DAYS OF GREAT EXPLORATION. WALKING THERE GIVES ME A SENSE OF THE UNIVERSE. OF WHO I AM. SOMETIMES IT HELPS.

SOMETIMES IT DOESN'T.
...BE GONE BEFORE ANYBODY NOTICES.

AND WHEN WE COME BACK, WE'LL BE HEROES! THE GIRLS WILL ALL BE LIKE, "OH, YOU'RE **REAL** RANGERS! **KISS** US!" AND THE TEACHERS WILL... WELL, **WHO CARES**?
THEY DON'T **DARE** SAY ANYTHING OR THEY KNOW MY DAD WILL RUIN THEM.

BUT TAKING A ROCKET? AND STEALING **SEVEN POUNDS** OF FLENNITE? SPRATT, THIS IS **SERIOUS**.
OF COURSE IT'S SERIOUS, LOWENGEAR. AND QUIT WHINING. YOU SOUND LIKE A TINY BABY EARTHER.
NOW ARE YOU IN OR NOT? ARE YOU COMING ALONG, OR ARE YOU GOING TO HIDE BENEATH YOUR BLANKETS AND SNIFFLE AND CRY?

I'M IN. I GUESS.
GOOD. LOAD UP THAT FLENNITE I LIBERATED. I'LL FIND STUCKERS AND WE'LL FIRE THIS ROCKET UP.
THIS IS GOING TO BE **EPIC**! PEOPLE WILL BE TALKING ABOUT ME FOR **MILLENNIA**!

beep!
INCOMING CALL.

BENSON! WHAT ARE YOU DOING TONIGHT? I'M OUT OF DETENTION! COME CELEBRATE!
SHHH!
I'LL TREAT YOU TO ICE CREAM AND SHOW YOU THE PROGRESS ON MY GAME! I'VE GOT THE FIRST DEEP SPHERE IMMERSION--
SHHH!!

WHY DO YOU KEEP SHUSHING US?
BECAUSE I'M HIDING!
I'M IN THE FEYNMAN SPACEPORT AND SPRATT AND HIS BULLY SQUAD ARE STEALING A SPACESHIP. AND SEVEN POUNDS OF FLENNITE!

SEVEN POUNDS?! THAT'S HOW MUCH THE ACADEMY ALLOCATES FOR A WHOLE YEAR! THAT'S INSANE!
YEAH. SPRATT WANTS TO GO DEEP SPACE EXPLORING.
SHOULD I... SHOULD I TELL SOMEONE?

YES!
NO!

HUH? HE HAS TO TELL. HE CAN'T LET SPRATT GET AWAY WITH THIS.
THERE'S NO WAY HE CAN TELL. SPRATT IS TOO WELL CONNECTED, AND BENSON STILL DOESN'T HAVE OFFICIAL STATUS, SINCE THE PAPERWORK HASN'T BEEN SIGNED.
HE'S THE ONE WHO'D GET IN TROUBLE FOR TELLING.

BENSON?
I'M LEAVING. IT'S NOT RIGHT TO TELL ON A FELLOW CADET.
I WON'T DO IT.

SMAKK!!
UNHH!

WON'T DO **WHAT**? WHAT WAS HE TALKING ABOUT?
DOESN'T MATTER, HE SAW US. WE'RE GOING TO HAVE TO DEAL WITH HIM.

YOU MEAN, **DEAL** WITH HIM?

NO. WE'RE JUST GOING TO HAVE TO TAKE HIM ALONG. THAT WAY, WE CAN MAKE SURE HE DOESN'T SCREW THINGS UP.

THESE OLD EXPLORATION ROCKETS, THEY HAVE HOLDING PENS FOR WHEN THE RANGERS FOUND NEW LIFE THEY WANTED TO TRANSPORT BACK TO THE KAYRUS ZOO.

AND THAT'S WHERE A STINKING **EARTHER** BELONGS.

IN A CAGE.
FZZWWT

DAY ONE HUNDRED AND TWENTY-ONE:
THE UNCERTAIN JOYS OF SOLITUDE.

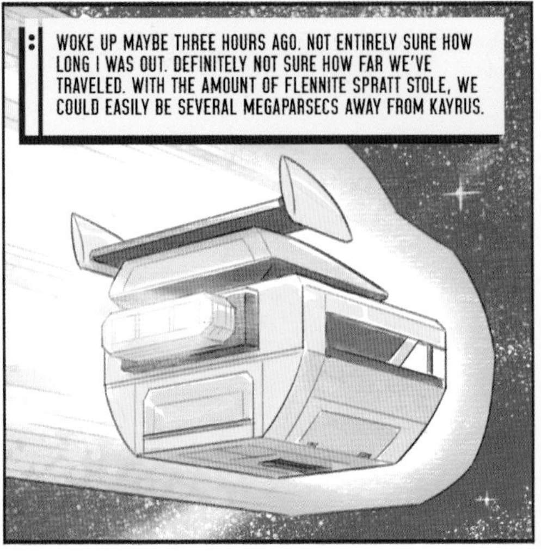
WOKE UP MAYBE THREE HOURS AGO. NOT ENTIRELY SURE HOW LONG I WAS OUT. DEFINITELY NOT SURE HOW FAR WE'VE TRAVELED. WITH THE AMOUNT OF FLENNITE SPRATT STOLE, WE COULD EASILY BE SEVERAL MEGAPARSECS AWAY FROM KAYRUS.

THEY MOST OFTEN LET ME OUT TO GO TO THE BATHROOM WHENEVER I BANG ON THE WALL. WE PROBABLY TRAVEL A FEW MILLION LIGHT YEARS BETWEEN MY BATHROOM BREAKS.

WE PROBABLY ROCKET A DISTANCE OF SIX OR SEVEN MEGAPARSECS BETWEEN THE TIMES WHEN THEY LET ME EAT THEIR LEFTOVERS.

BUT WE ONLY TRAVEL MAYBE TEN FEET BETWEEN THE TIMES THEY INSULT ME. IT'S PRETTY MUCH CONSTANT. I GUESS I'M AMUSING OR SOMETHING. THEY'VE TAKEN TO CALLING MY ROOM THE ZOO. THEIR LEVEL OF WIT IS ASTOUNDING.
DOES IT DO TRICKS? I WONDER IF IT CAN TALK?
MAKE SURE TO WEAR A FULL HAZMAT SUIT IF YOU GO INTO THE ZOO. EARTHERS HAVE ALL SORTS OF DISEASES.

LET'S GO **FASTER**! **BURN** SOME MORE OF THAT FLENNITE! LET'S BREAK SPEED RECORDS!
HA HA HA HA!
I WONDER IF THEY'VE FORGOTTEN THAT SHIP LOGS WILL RECORD EVERYTHING THAT HAPPENS ABOARD THIS VESSEL, OR IF THEY'RE JUST TOO STUPID TO CARE?

DAY ONE HUNDRED AND TWENTY-TWO: ANOTHER DAY OF CAPTIVITY. THE ROAR OF THE ROCKETS IS A CONSTANT. IN SOME WAYS I LIKE IT, SINCE IT LULLS ME TO SLEEP. ON THE OTHER HAND, I CAN'T BELIEVE THE VALUABLE RESOURCES SPRATT IS BURNING UP, ALL FOR WHAT AMOUNTS TO A JOYRIDE.

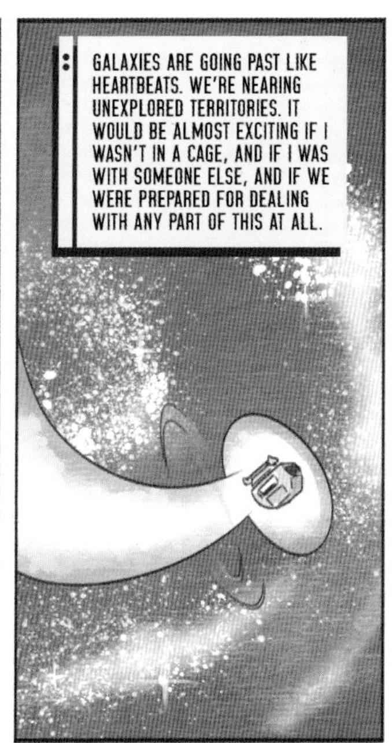
GALAXIES ARE GOING PAST LIKE HEARTBEATS. WE'RE NEARING UNEXPLORED TERRITORIES. IT WOULD BE ALMOST EXCITING IF I WASN'T IN A CAGE, AND IF I WAS WITH SOMEONE ELSE, AND IF WE WERE PREPARED FOR DEALING WITH ANY PART OF THIS AT ALL.

BATHROOM BREAK, BENSON.

HEY, DUMBO.
THAT'S THE LEVEL OF INSULTS YOU GOT TODAY?
USE UP ALL YOUR WIT YESTERDAY, THE WAY YOU'RE USING UP ALL THIS **FLENNITE**?

NO ANSWER FROM SPRATT AT ALL? SOMETHING'S WRONG. HE LOOKS WORRIED. I'D BE AMUSED IF I WASN'T TRAPPED ABOARD THE SAME SHIP HE IS, ON THE EDGES OF THE KNOWN UNIVERSE.
C'MON, TO THE BATHROOMS, THEN BACK TO YOUR CELL.

DAY ONE HUNDRED AND TWENTY-THREE: DAY THREE OF CAPTIVITY. AS MUCH AS I'VE BEEN ENJOYING MY WIDE RANGE OF ACTIVITIES, LIKE, "GOING TO THE BATHROOM" AND "EATING LEFTOVER SCRAPS" AND "NOTHING ELSE," I HAVE TO SAY TODAY HAS BEEN INTERESTING.

THE MOOD I'VE BEEN SEEING IN THE SHIP IS FAR LESS JOVIAL THAN ON THE FIRST DAY. LOT OF TENSION OUT THERE, NOW.
MY MATH IS FINE.
MAYBE IF YOU HADN'T BEEN FIRING OFF FLENNITE LIKE FIREWORKS, IT WOULD BE EASIER TO CALCULATE OUR CURRENT POSITION.
PISS OFF, LOWENGEAR. YOU SHOULD HAVE HAD US TO THE HALWALL RIFT BY NOW, BUT INSTEAD YOU KEEP WHINING LIKE AN ITTY-BITTY BABY.

SO FIGURE OUT WHERE WE ARE, AND GET US BACK ON TRACK, AND QUIT FREAKING OUT.
YOU SOUND AS DUMB AS BENSON.

YOU KNOW, HE'S NOT ALL THAT DUMB.
HE'S TOP OF THE CLASS IN NAVIGATION, BESIDES THE EMILY TWINS, OF COURSE.

OH SHUT UP. YOU WANT TO GET IN THAT CAGE WITH HIM?
DO YOU?
ANSWER ME!

DAY ONE HUNDRED AND TWENTY-FOUR:
DAY FOUR OF CAPTIVITY.
COME ON. I'LL TAKE YOU TO THE BATHROOM, BENSON.
MAYBE THE MAP'S **WRONG**!

HOW THE CRAP WOULD I KNOW? MAYBE YOU THINK **YOU** CAN DO BETTER?!
MAYBE YOU SHOULD QUIT YELLING AT ME. RIGHT NOW.

OR **WHAT**? I GOT BAD NEWS, SPRATT! THAT'S THE **UNIVERSE** OUT THERE, AND IT DOESN'T CARE THAT YOUR **DADDY** IS IMPORTANT!
A **COOL FAMILY NAME** DOESN'T MEAN YOU CAN BEND TIME AND SPACE UNTIL WE KNOW WHERE WE ARE, OR UNTIL **YOU'RE** NOT A **COMPLETE JERK**!
MAYBE YOU SHOULD **SHUT UP**, STUCKERS, OR I **SWEAR** I'LL SHOVE THIS STAR CHART DOWN YOUR **STUPID THROAT**!

YEAH? REALLY?
CAN YOU DO THAT ALL BY YOURSELF, OR DO YOU NEED YOUR DADDY TO HOLD YOUR HAND?

AFTER YOU'RE THROUGH IN THE BATHROOM, I'LL SEE WHAT I CAN DO ABOUT GETTING YOU A MEAL.
NO MORE LEFTOVERS, EITHER. I'LL GET YOU SOMETHING **REAL** TO EAT, THIS TIME, BENSON.

DAY ONE HUNDRED AND TWENTY-FIVE: DEALING WITH DEVILS.

SO... HERE'S THE DEAL.

WE'RE RUNNING OUT OF SUPPLIES, AND WE DON'T KNOW WHERE WE ARE. NONE OF THE STAR CHARTS MATCH.
ALSO, SPRATT'S BEEN BLOWING THROUGH THE FLENNITE, AND WE'RE NOT SURE WE HAVE ENOUGH TO GET BACK TO OCCUPIED SPACE, LET ALONE THE KAYRUS ACADEMY.

AND BESIDES THE EMILY TWINS, YOU WERE TOPS IN OUR CLASS IN NAVIGATION, SO WE WERE WONDERING IF YOU COULD HELP US CHART A--
IF WE DON'T MAKE IT HOME, YOU DON'T EITHER, SO DO SOMETHING, TRASH!

I WAS SUPPOSED TO DO ALL THE TALKING.

BUT HE'S RIGHT ABOUT--
OKAY.

I'LL HELP.

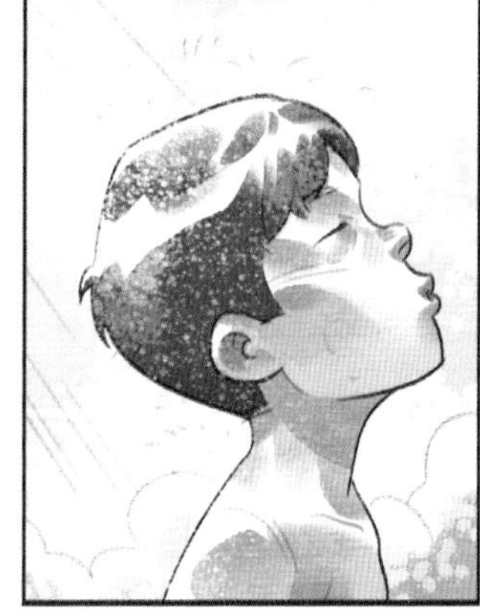
THE FIRST THING I DO IS TAKE A SHOWER, BECAUSE IT CLEARS MY MIND. ALTHOUGH, COME TO THINK OF IT, IF I WAS CRUEL I'D MAKE THEM PUT UP WITH MY FIVE-DAY STINK.

NEXT, THERE'S THE QUESTION OF SUPPLIES.
LET ME GET THIS STRAIGHT, YOU THREE THOUGHT YOU'D EXPLORE HALF THE UNIVERSE, BUT YOU ONLY BROUGHT ENOUGH FOOD FOR A WEEK?
IT WAS HIS JOB TO GET SUPPLIES.
MINE? WHAT DUTIES DID YOU HAVE? JUST ORDERING US AROUND? YOU SEEM TO HAVE A HUGE SUPPLY OF THAT!

BICKERING ISN'T GOING TO HELP ANYTHING. WE'RE GOING TO HAVE TO PUT EVERYONE ON RATIONS.
I'M MAKING UP A SCHEDULE. WE'LL STRETCH THE FOOD OUT FOR AT LEAST ANOTHER WEEK.
ARE YOU CRAZY, HOW CAN WE LIVE ON THAT?

LOOK, I STUDIED SUPPLY MANAGEMENT, NOT MAGICAL CREATION OF FOOD, SO UNLESS YOU HAPPEN TO HAVE A MAGIC WAND, QUIT WASTING CALORIES COMPLAINING.

IT'S ONLY FOUR HOURS LATER THAT WE CAUGHT STUCKERS HOARDING FOOD.
WHAT THE HECK, STUCKERS?
I WAS HUNGRY! I'M NOT SOME STUPID HUMAN THAT'S--

HE RANTED FOR A LONG TIME, MAKING IT AN EVEN EASIER DECISION TO PUT HIM IN CRYO-STASIS.
SO, WITH HIM ON ICE, WE CAN EAT MORE NOW?
NO. BUT THIS SHOULD ADD A COUPLE DAYS BEFORE WE RUN OUT OF FOOD.

THE HARDEST DECISION WAS SHUTTING DOWN THE QUANTUM COMMUNICATOR.
BENSON, LISTEN, WE CAN'T SHUT THAT OFF.
THIS FAR OUT, THAT'S THE **ONLY** WAY WE HAVE OF CONTACTING ANYONE, AT LEAST WITHOUT IT TAKING CENTURIES.

I KNOW, BUT DO YOU KNOW HOW MUCH ENERGY THIS THING TAKES?
YOU THREE BURNT THROUGH THE FLENNITE SO QUICKLY THAT... IF WE FIRE THIS THING UP... IT WILL CHEW UP ALMOST THE ENTIRE REMAINING SUPPLY.
IF WE MAKE A CALL FOR HELP, WE **STRAND** OURSELVES, AND WE **CAN'T** RELY ON ANYONE FINDING US.

YEAH, WHATEVER. BUT--
BUT **NOTHING**. YOU'RE LIKE A BABY CRYING FOR HELP, BUT HELP IS TOO FAR AWAY TO HEAR US.
SO **GROW UP**, AND LEARN TO **WALK**, SO WE CAN DEAL WITH THIS **OURSELVES**.

ALL NONESSENTIAL EQUIPMENT IS TO BE SHUT DOWN IMMEDIATELY. WE'RE GOING WITH ENGINES AND LIFE SUPPORT **ONLY**.
HOW ABOUT THE **REFRIGERATOR**, IDIOT? YOU WANT ALL THE FOOD TO SPOIL?

NO. LOOK AROUND, SPRATT. WE'RE TWO STEPS AWAY FROM THE BIGGEST REFRIGERATOR IN EXISTENCE.
AND IF YOU DON'T FEEL LIKE STORING YOUR FOOD **OUTSIDE**, NO PROBLEM.

"KEEP IT WITH STUCKERS."

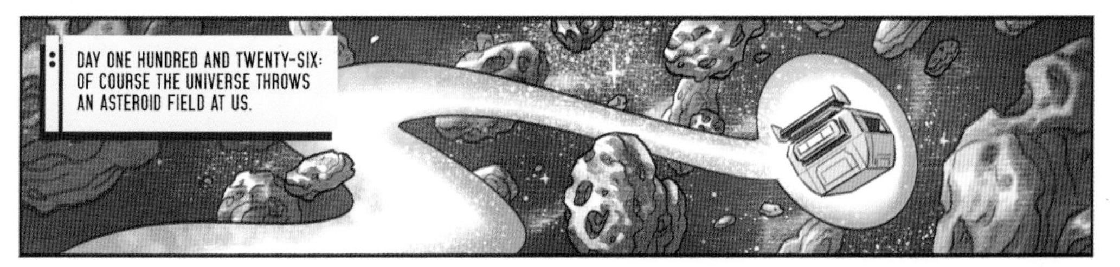
DAY ONE HUNDRED AND TWENTY-SIX: OF COURSE THE UNIVERSE THROWS AN ASTEROID FIELD AT US.

IT WOULD BE EASIER TO NAVIGATE THIS IF YOU'D STOP SCREAMING!
OF COURSE I'M SCREAMING, IDIOT! WE'RE GONNA DIE! YOU TURNED OFF THE AUTOMATIC AVOIDANCE CONTROL SYSTEM!

WE'RE NOT GOING TO DIE!
I CAN FLY US THROUGH THIS!
JUST LET ME CONCENTRATE!

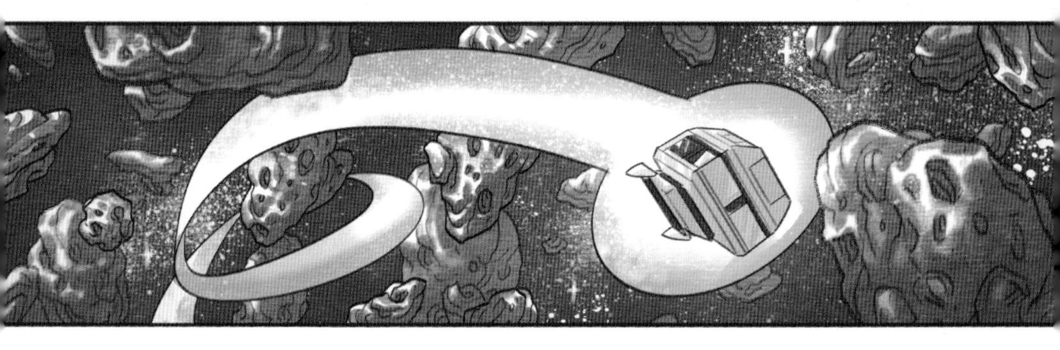

I CAN DO THIS. I CAN GET US THROUGH THESE ASTEROIDS. IT'S NO MORE DIFFICULT THAN RUNNING THROUGH A BISON-REX STAMPEDE BACK ON EARTH.

JUST STAY ALERT.

JUST WATCH OUT FOR THE HORNS. AND THE HOOVES. THE CLAWS. AND THE TEETH.

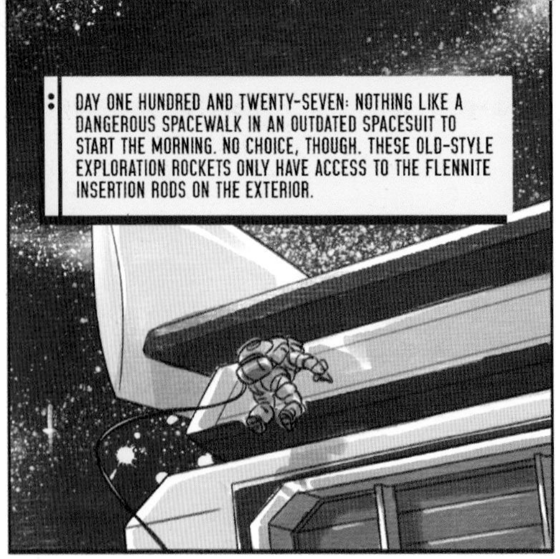
DAY ONE HUNDRED AND TWENTY-SEVEN: NOTHING LIKE A DANGEROUS SPACEWALK IN AN OUTDATED SPACESUIT TO START THE MORNING. NO CHOICE, THOUGH. THESE OLD-STYLE EXPLORATION ROCKETS ONLY HAVE ACCESS TO THE FLENNITE INSERTION RODS ON THE EXTERIOR.

AND I NEED A SAMPLE. JUST A SPECK.

TELL ME AGAIN WHAT YOU'RE DOING?
I'M MAKING A MATERIAL TUNER. IT'S AN OLD MINING TRICK I READ ABOUT DURING MY STUDIES. IT'S BASICALLY ANCIENT HISTORY, BUT MAYBE OUR ONLY HOPE.

WHAT I'M DOING IS FLOODING NEUTRINOS THROUGH THE FLENNITE PARTICLE, CREATING A RESONANCE FLUCTUATION AROUND THE FLENNITE'S EXACT VIBRATION LEVEL.
BASICALLY, I'M MAKING IT SING.

AND THEN WE'LL USE CHESHIRE HERE TO TUNE INTO THE SAME FREQUENCY COMING FROM SPACE, AND THAT WILL HOPEFULLY LEAD US TO ENOUGH FLENNITE TO GET US HOME.
IT'LL BE LIKE FOLLOWING A GIANT MUSICAL COBWEB THROUGH SPACE, ALL THE WAY BACK TO THE CENTER OF THE WEB, AND TO THE SPIDER. OR THE FLENNITE, IN THIS CASE.

IF YOU THINK THAT WILL WORK, YOU'RE THE DUMBEST PERSON I'VE EVER KNOWN.

YAY, TEAM.

BUT IF THIS MACHINE I MADE DOESN'T WORK THE WAY I *HOPE*, IF WE *DON'T* FIND THE FLENNITE, THEN WE'LL ABSOLUTELY BE STRANDED FOR SURE. I MEAN, A HUNDRED PERCENT CHANCE OF DYING OUT HERE.

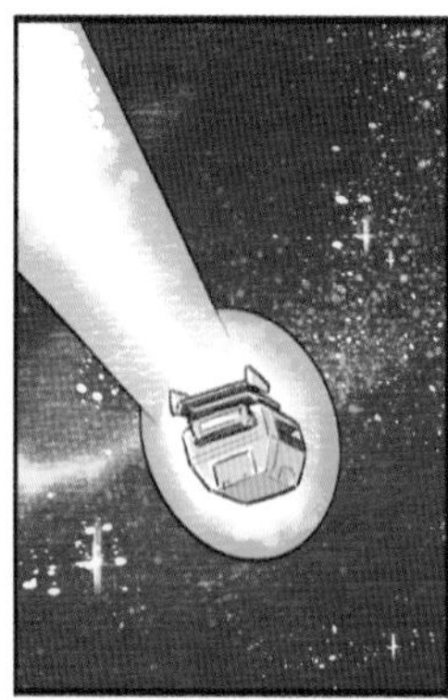

WE'RE OFF TO FIND THE FLENNITE, HOPEFULLY.

USING THE PRECIOUS RESERVES OF WHAT WE ALREADY HAVE.

IT'S A GAMBLE.

BUT I GUESS THAT'S WHAT A RANGER'S LIFE IS ABOUT.

THE SAD THING IS...

... FOLLOWING THIS MUSICAL THREAD THROUGH SPACE...

... WE'RE PASSING GALAXIES THAT NO ONE'S EVER EXPLORED.

IT'S HARD NOT TO WONDER WHAT'S OUT THERE, ORBITING ALL THOSE SUNS.

MAYBE THERE ARE OTHER CIVILIZATIONS.

MAYBE THERE'S NOTHING.

EACH PLANET IS A ROLL OF THE DICE.

BUT THEY USUALLY COME UP EMPTY.

THIS ISN'T WORKING. YOU'RE GETTING US KILLED.

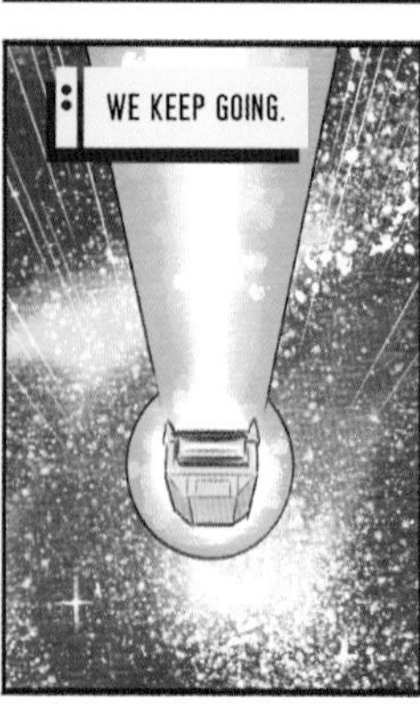
WE KEEP GOING.

I USED TO LOVE GETTING LOST IN THE WOODS NEXT TO OUR FARM.

THERE'S A CERTAIN PEACE TO NOT KNOWING WHERE YOU ARE.

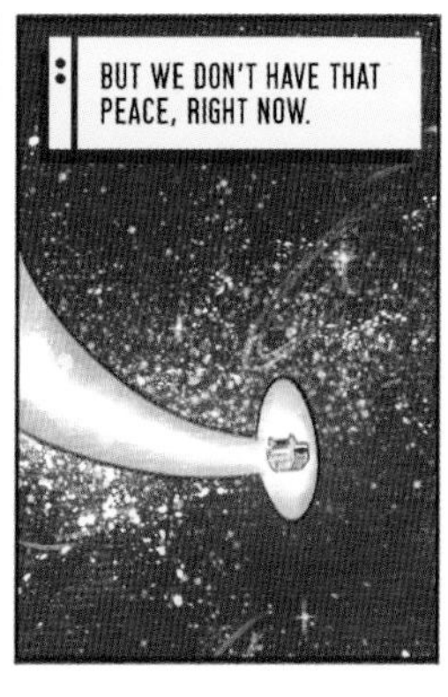
BUT WE DON'T HAVE THAT PEACE, RIGHT NOW.

THE SIGNAL *SEEMS* STRONG, BUT WE *SHOULD* HAVE FOUND IT BY NOW. THIS ISN'T WORKING.

AND THEY KNOW IT.

ALL WE NEED IS *ONE* PIECE OF FLENNITE. IT'S *INCREDIBLY* POWERFUL.

A CHUNK THE SIZE OF A WALNUT WOULD DO.

THE *BIGGEST* PIECE EVER FOUND WAS THE SIZE OF A WATERMELON.

BUT WE JUST NEED THAT WALNUT.

WE NEED TO FIND THAT WALNUT IN ALL OF SPACE.

WE JUST NEED TO FOLLOW THE MUSIC.

OR ELSE WE'RE STRANDED. DOOMED.

I MISS DAD. AND MY SISTER, LILA. AND MY STUPID, WONDERFUL DOG.

I MISS MILKING THE COWS. DOING MY CHORES. HOW'S THAT EVEN *POSSIBLE*?

I MISS SORAYA. I MISS THE WAY SHE--

FLENNITE DETECTED. OBJECTIVE ATTAINED.
WHAT?

WHOA.

WHOA.

A SIMPLE SPACEWALK GETS US ENOUGH FLENNITE TO FIRE THE ENGINES AS MUCH AS WE WANT.

AND MORE THAN ENOUGH TO REOPEN THE Q-PHONE AND CALL HOME.
YES. YOU HEARD ME CORRECTLY. WE'RE IN QUADRANT 456-21-UV-12, AND WE JUST DISCOVERED A FLENNITE ASTEROID.
YES. THE ENTIRE ASTEROID IS FLENNITE. TWENTY-THREE THOUSAND TONS OF MATERIAL.
YES. I'M SURE OF THE CALCULATIONS.

BOY, **LISTEN** TO ME. BENSON, ARE YOU LISTENING?
YES, SIR. I CAN HEAR--
LAY CLAIM TO THAT ASTEROID **NOW**, IN THE NAME OF THE KAYRUS ACADEMY.

DO YOU REALIZE HOW MUCH THAT'S WORTH? UNTOLD TRILLIONS. TRILLIONS OF TRILLIONS, EVEN. YOU COULD BUY AND SELL ENTIRE SOLAR SYSTEMS WITH THAT.
THE KAYRUS ACADEMY WOULD BE UNQUESTIONABLY THE RICHEST ORGANIZATION IN EXISTENCE.

WE COULD EXPAND IN WAYS UNHEARD OF. THE ERA OF SPACE EXPLORATION WILL BEGIN ANEW.
BENSON... CLAIM THAT ASTEROID IN THE NAME OF THE KAYRUS ACADEMY, UNDER GALACTIC LAW. DO IT **RIGHT NOW**.

BENSON, DO YOU--
SORRY, SIR. WE MUST BE ENTERING A GRAVITATIONAL WARP. PROBABLY A BLACK HOLE NEARBY. LOSING CONTACT.
I'LL CALL AGAIN WHEN WE'RE CLEAR.

CHESHIRE, CAN YOU USE SOME FLENNITE TO HEIGHTEN YOUR CALL RANGE? CONTACT MY HOUSE ON EARTH?
AFFIRMATIVE.

NOW, BY PURE LUCK, I FOUND SOMETHING, AND THE KAYRUS ACADEMY WANTS IT. IT'S AN ASTEROID. PURE FLENNITE. BUT, DO I **GIVE** IT TO THEM?

IT DOESN'T FEEL RIGHT TO GIVE IT TO THEM AFTER ALL THE MESS I'VE BEEN THROUGH, WHICH IS, BELIEVE ME, PRETTY MESSY FROM THEIR SIDE.

THE THING IS, IT FEELS WRONG TO EVEN CONSIDER DOING ANYTHING ELSE. I'M A KAYRUS CADET. THAT **SHOULD** STAND FOR SOMETHING.

IT **WOULD** HAVE STOOD FOR SOMETHING IN THE DAYS OF KANNON JRLL, OR DRRG OF PENN.

... HE ALWAYS KNOWS THE RIGHT THING TO SAY.

ALL YOU HAVE TO DO IS REPEAT AFTER ME. WE'RE BEAMING THIS TO THE LEGAL DEPARTMENT.
GOT IT, DIRECTOR SQUA-TRONT, GO AHEAD.

I, CADET BENSON CHOW, ON THIS DAY OF OCTOBER 7, 3115...
I, CADET BENSON CHOW, ON THIS DAY OF OCTOBER 7, 3115...

HEREBY CLAIM THIS FLENNITE ASTEROID IN ACCORDANCE WITH GALACTIC LAW 47-23V OF THE FEDERATION DEEP SPACE MINING CODE.

...OF THE FEDERATION DEEP SPACE MINING CODE.

GOOD, NOW... PLANT THE FLAG.

WELL DONE, BENSON. THAT FLAG HAS A REGISTRATION CODE EMBEDDED, SO NOW THERE CAN BE NO MISTAKE.
SHUNKK!
THE FLENNITE ASTEROID, THANKS TO YOUR LEGAL CLAIM AS OUR CADET, NOW BELONGS TO THE KAYRUS ACADEMY.

POP!

I THOUGHT WE WERE STILL RATIONING?
IT'S OKAY, LOWENGEAR. IT'S TRUE WE CAN'T MOVE FULL SPEED WHILE TOWING THE ASTEROID...
...BUT WE **CAN** FIRE THE ENGINES PRETTY WELL, AND NOW THAT WE'RE IN COMMUNICATION AGAIN, IT WON'T BE A PROBLEM TO HAVE AN ESCORT MEET US HALFWAY.

OH. COOL. WELL THEN... CHEERS TO EVERYONE!
YOU TOO, STUCKERS.
CLINK

WELL ISN'T **THIS** NICE.
I GUESS YOU GUYS ARE FRIENDS, NOW THAT EVERYTHING'S OKAY, BUT LET'S NOT FORGET THAT BENSON IS THE ONE WHO GOT US INTO THIS MESS IN THE FIRST PLACE.
ME?

TO BE FAIR TO BENSON, WE **DID** BEAT HIM UP AND KIDNAP HIM.
ALSO, AGAIN TO BE FAIR, WHAT THE HECK DO YOU MEAN IT'S **HIS** FAULT? WHAT DID **HE** DO?

IT'S NOT IMPORTANT WHAT HE DID! IT'S IMPORTANT WHAT YOU'RE DOING!
YOU'RE SUPPOSED TO BE **MY** FRIEND, AND DO WHAT **I** TELL YOU!
BUT I DON'T REMEMBER TELLING YOU TO MAKE **FRIENDS** WITH SOME **LOWBORN EARTH MAGGOT** WHO COULDN'T--

WHAMM!!
HUH?
AHHH!

WHAT THE HECK?

ALARM! ALARM! THIS VESSEL IS UNDER ATTACK! ALARM! ALARM! ENEMY VESSEL IS TWO HUNDRED YARDS AWAY! ALARM! ALARM!

THIS ISN'T POSSIBLE! WE HAVE A GILLARI-4X EARLY WARNING SYSTEM! WE SHOULD BE ABLE TO DETECT POTENTIAL THREATS FROM A THOUSAND MILES AWAY!
HOW'D THEY GET SO CLOSE?!

BECAUSE WE HACKED INTO YOUR SYSTEM.

FRANKLY, YOU MADE IT PRETTY EASY, SINCE YOU'RE RUNNING AN OUTDATED SYSTEM THAT'S FULL OF HOLES.
AND, LET'S FACE IT, YOU WEREN'T HARD TO FIND, NOT WITH THE WAY YOU...

"...WENT AND **BLASTED** YOUR MESSAGE TO THE KAYRUS ACADEMY WITH ALL THAT **POWER** OF THE FLENNITE ASTEROID. IT WAS LIKE A BELLOWING SHOUT IN THE SILENCE OF SPACE. WE COULDN'T **HELP** BUT OVERHEAR YOU!"

WHAT I'M TRYING TO SAY HERE IS... WE KNOW WHAT YOU FOUND. AND WE'LL BE TAKING IT, FOR SURE.

IT'S PIRATES FROM THE BOOSH FEDERATION.
FROM THE **WHAT**?

THE BOOSH PIRATE FEDERATION. A COLLECTION OF SCAVENGERS. MURDERERS. BASED IN THE ALBIREO SYSTEM NEAR FINGOLIN. THOUSANDS OF SHIPS. INCLUDING A CAPTURED DESTROYER CLASS VESSEL FROM THE STRAAIANS.

THE BOOSH ARE THE ONES RESPONSIBLE FOR THE ATTACK ON BANTOCK.

THEY'RE THE ONES WHO TOOK OVER EIGHTY THOUSAND HOSTAGES DURING THE CHOLLIAN CRISIS.

THEY SCOUR THE SPACEWAYS, PREYING ON UNESCORTED VESSELS.

THE BOOSH ARE THE ONES WHO OBLITERATED THE HUSCOET PEACE DELEGATION.

AND LEFT EIGHTY THOUSAND HOSTAGES TO STARVE TO DEATH DURING THE AFTERMATH OF THE CHOLLIAN CRISIS.

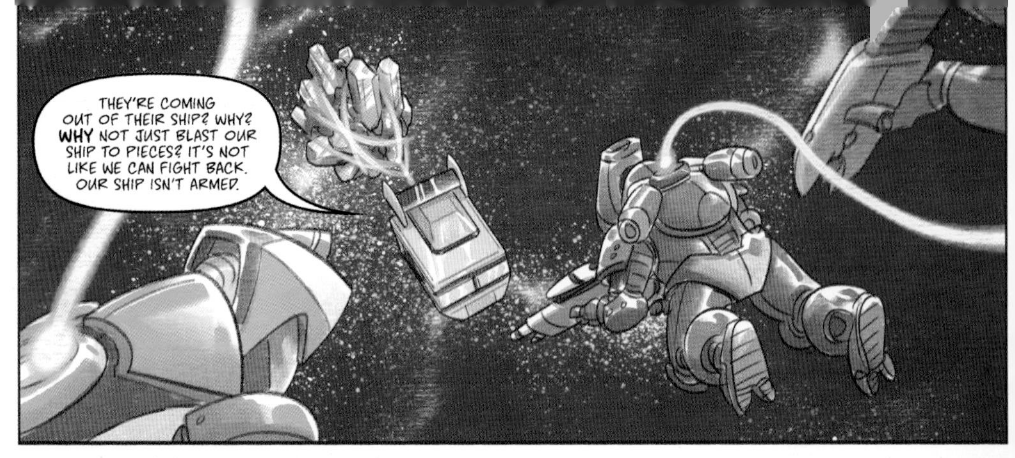
THEY'RE COMING OUT OF THEIR SHIP? WHY? WHY NOT JUST BLAST OUR SHIP TO PIECES? IT'S NOT LIKE WE CAN FIGHT BACK. OUR SHIP ISN'T ARMED.

BECAUSE THEY CAN'T BLOW UP OUR SHIP WITHOUT POSSIBLY BLOWING UP THE FLENNITE.

WISELY SAID, OH DOOMED CHILDREN. SO WE'LL JUST BOARD YOU AND TAKE COMMAND OF YOUR VESSEL. EASILY ENOUGH DONE.
WHICH MEANS YOU GET A CHOICE: YOU CAN EITHER JOIN US, OR YOU CAN GET TOSSED OUT INTO SPACE LIKE THE DEBRIS.

WHAT ARE YOU DOING?
CHOOSING THE THIRD OPTION. GOING OUT TO FIGHT THEM. OUR SHIP ISN'T ARMED, BUT WE HAVE A LASER PISTOL. I CAN FIGHT.
AREN'T YOU AFRAID?

COURSE I AM. BUT I'M REMEMBERING SOMETHING I LEARNED LONG AGO.
COURAGE ISN'T ABOUT THE LACK OF FEAR. IT'S ABOUT DECIDING THAT SOMETHING ELSE IS MORE IMPORTANT THAN YOUR FEAR.

AND SOMETIMES IT'S BETTER TO BE AFRAID WHILE FIGHTING, RATHER THAN AFRAID WHILE HIDING.

THE PIRATES ARE USING A JAMMER. SHUTTING DOWN OUR ENGINES, DISABLING NOT ONLY OUR VESSEL, BUT OUR JETPACKS, TOO. IT'S A GOOD MOVE ON THEIR PART, EVEN THOUGH IT MEANS THEIR OWN JETPACKS ARE SEVERELY LIMITED, BECAUSE THEY'RE IN THE FIELD OF EFFECT.
BUT MY SUIT IS SO OLD THAT IT WORKS ON DIFFERENT TECHNOLOGY. IT'S SO OUTDATED THAT... IT STILL WORKS. SOMETIMES THE CLASSICS ARE BEST.
HEY! HOW'S HE STILL DOING THAT?
IT GIVES ME A LOT MORE MANEUVERABILITY, WHILE THEY HAVE TO DEAL WITH TETHERS FOR THEIR POWER. SO, YOU KNOW, EVERYTHING IS GOING GREAT. NO PROBLEMS HERE!
WHO CARES WHY HIS SUIT'S STILL WORKING?
PUT A LASER THROUGH HIS FACE, AND THEN HE WON'T BE WORKING!

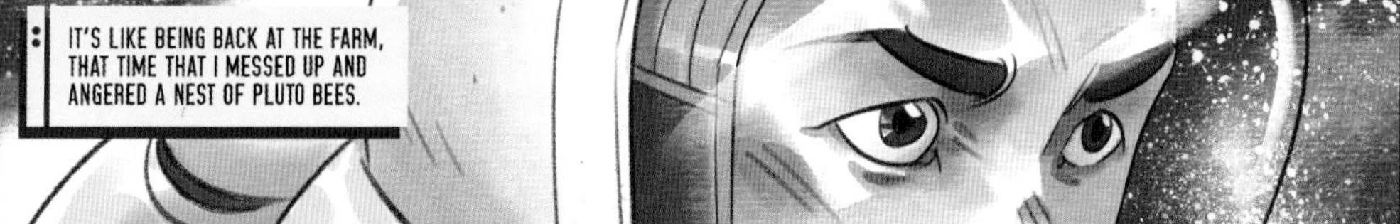
IT'S LIKE BEING BACK AT THE FARM, THAT TIME THAT I MESSED UP AND ANGERED A NEST OF PLUTO BEES.

BACK THEN I JUST HAD TO DODGE ALL THE BEES UNTIL I COULD KNOCK OUT THE QUEEN BEE, BECAUSE THEY HAVE A COLLECTIVE MIND.

BAPP!!

THIS TIME, SAME DRILL. EXCEPT THAT IF A LASER HITS ME, IT'S A LOT WORSE THAN EVEN A PARALYZING PLUTO BEE STING. AND INSTEAD OF PUNCHING A BEE IN THE CHIN, I'M TRYING TO LINE UP A SHOT TO TAKE DOWN A PIRATE.

NOT YET.

NOT QUITE YET. ALMOST HAD A SHOT, THERE.

AND... IF HE MOVES TO THE RIGHT, THAT WILL GIVE ME TIME TO...
FZZZZ

YES!
KOWW!!

NICE TRY, **KID**, BUT OUR ADVANCED SUITS CAN HANDLE A LOT MORE THAN THAT LITTLE BITTY LASER OF YOURS.
SO WHY DON'T YOU JUST SAVE US ALL SOME TIME AND LET US BLOW YOUR **STUPID** HEAD OFF?

OKAY. NEXT PLAN. ANOTHER ONE THAT REMINDS ME OF BEING BACK ON THE FARM. THE NEIGHBORS HAD A DOG. HE WAS MEAN AS A BLACK HOLE SKUNK. SOME PEOPLE ARE JUST BAD. SOME DOGS, TOO.

ZZZSSSS

ZZZT!
HUH?

ONE BY ONE, I SEVER THEIR TETHERS.
ZZZSSS
ZZZSSS

SENDING THEM ADRIFT.
DAMN IT!

AND THEIR MOMENTUM CARRIES THEM OFF INTO SPACE.

I BOUGHT US SOME TIME! LET'S GET ROLLING! HURRY!
WE SHOULD BE ABLE TO OVERPOWER THEIR JAMMING SIGNALS, BECAUSE WE HAVE LITERALLY TONS OF FLENNITE POWER TO DRAW FROM!
REROUTE OUR SYSTEMS THROUGH THE FLENNITE CORE AND FIRE IT UP HARD!
MY PLAN IS... BY THE TIME THE BOOSH RECOVER, WE'LL HAVE OUR ENGINES BACK ON LINE. IF WE CAN DO THAT, THEN WE'LL BE LONG GONE.

ARE WE MAKING PROGRESS?
NOT ENOUGH!
THE ENGINES ARE REALLY GRINDING BETWEEN THE JAMMING SIGNALS AND ALL THE FLENNITE WE'RE CHANNELING! WE **CAN'T** PUSH THEM MUCH HARDER. THEY'LL **OVERLOAD**!

OKAY, I'M HERE, NOW! GET OUT OF THE CHAIR!
WHAT? **NO WAY**! I'M THE BOSS!
NOW'S NOT THE TIME FOR YOUR HISSY FIT, SPRATT!

YOU GOT US INTO THIS!
WHAT ARE YOU **DOING**, SPRATT?
WE **DON'T** HAVE TIME FOR THIS!

IF THE BOOSH GET BACK IN THAT SHIP, I HAVE A FEELING THEY WON'T GO EASY ON US, THIS TIME. THEY'LL BLAST US INTO PIECES, AND COLLECT THE FLENNITE REMNANTS AFTERWARD.

I BARELY EVEN KNOW WHAT'S HAPPENING. ALL I KNOW IS THAT I'M DOWN ON THE FLOOR, AND SPRATT IS PUNCHING ME, AND I'M THINKING OF HOW STUPID THIS ALL IS, AND THAT MAYBE SPRATT IS INSANE, AND I'M ALSO THINKING OF THE FARM, OF TEACHING MY SISTER HOW TO TIE UP AN ANGRY CALF.

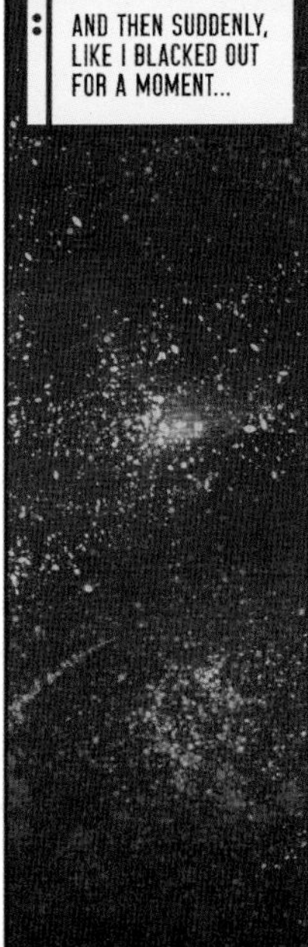
AND THEN SUDDENLY, LIKE I BLACKED OUT FOR A MOMENT...

...THINGS HAVE CHANGED, AND SPRATT IS ALL TIED UP LIKE A CALF, EXCEPT INSTEAD OF ROPE IT'S A METAL SPACEWALK WIRE.
AND **THAT'S** HOW YOU DO IT, LILA!
HUH? WHO'S **LILA**?

UH. MY SISTER. CAN WE PRETEND I DIDN'T SAY THAT?
SURE, AND, WOW, THE WAY YOU HANDLED SPRATT WAS **AWESOME**.

THANKS. NOW, HOW CAN WE SPEED UP OUR ENGINES?
NOT SURE WE **CAN**. IF IT WAS JUST A MATTER OF OVERCOMING THEIR JAMMER, WE'D HAVE MORE THAN ENOUGH POWER, THANKS TO THE FLENNITE. BUT THE PROBLEM IS...

"...WE HAVE TO **KEEP** OVERCOMING THE SIGNAL. LIKE, WE BREAK DOWN ONE WALL, AND THEIR SIGNAL PUTS UP ANOTHER.
"DOESN'T MATTER THAT WE'RE POWERFUL ENOUGH TO BREAK THROUGH THE WALLS, NOT IF THEY'RE INFINITE."

PREPARE AN OMNI-BURST! FOCUS ON THE **BRIDGE** OF THEIR SHIP! I DON'T EVEN WANT ATOMS LEFT!
WHEEE-OOO! WE'RE HAVING SOME FUN TODAY, BOYS!

ANY IDEAS?
WELL, IF YOU KNOW HOW TO BOOST THE POWER OF YOUR LASER PISTOL BY LIKE, **TEN THOUSAND TIMES**, WE MIGHT HAVE A CHANCE, BUT OTHERWISE...
HMM. I KNOW YOU MEANT THAT AS A JOKE, BUT WITH A FLENNITE BOOST MAYBE WE COULD ACTUALLY...

WARNING. ENEMY SHIP HAS LOCKED ITS TARGETING SYSTEM. THEIR WEAPONS WILL FIRE IN FOUR SECONDS.
OH **CRAP**!

OH **COME ON**! I NEED AT LEAST FIVE MINUTES TO REWIRE THIS THING!
THREE SECONDS.

DO ONE OF YOUR TRICKS! **DO ONE OF YOUR TRICKS!**
I'M ALL OUT OF TRICKS, HERE. NOT EVEN THE BROKEN BROTHERS OF THE FOG COULD MAKE TIME STAND STILL!
TWO SECONDS.

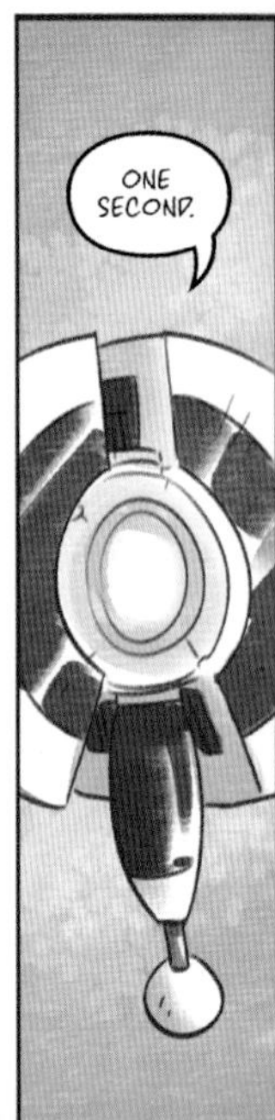
ONE SECOND.

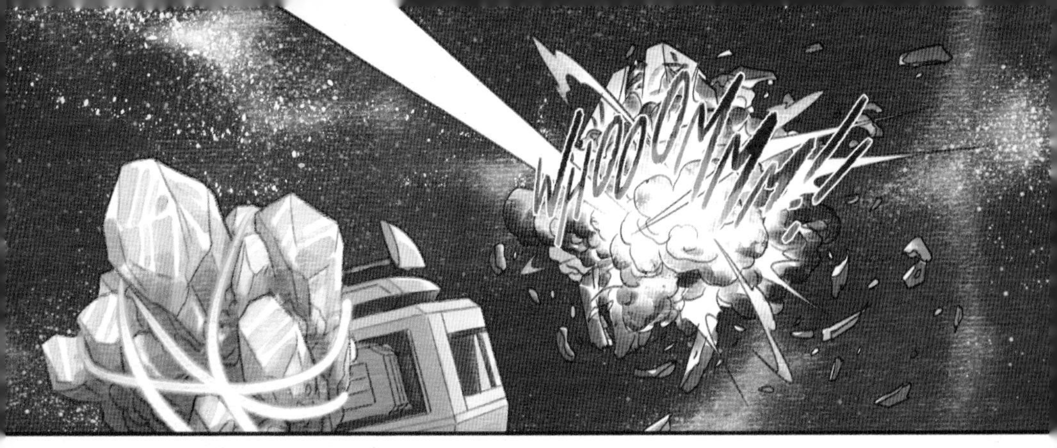
WHOOOMMM!

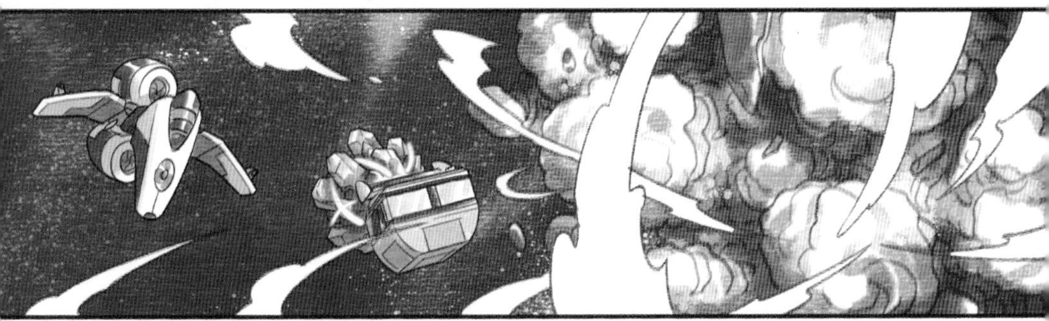

WHAT JUST HAPPENED?

HEY, ROOMIE!
BOGLEY?

WE'RE HERE, TOO!
SORAYA! LORNA!

ARE YOU OKAY, BENSON? I'M COMING OVER!
YOU BETTER BE OKAY OR I WILL KICK YOUR EARTH BEHIND!

BENSON! YOU'RE **OKAY**!

SPRATT?
UH, LONG STORY.
IT'S NOT THAT LONG OF STORY. SPRATT WAS BEING **SPRATT**, SO BENSON TIED HIM UP. END OF STORY.

WHATEVER! I'M JUST GLAD YOU'RE OKAY!
BUT, HOW ARE YOU EVEN **HERE**? HOW'D YOU **FIND** ME?

OH, IT WASN'T HARD. THE WHOLE SCHOOL IS BUZZING ABOUT YOUR FIND, AND SINCE I HAD A GENERAL IDEA OF WHERE YOU WERE...
...WE JUST LIBERATED A SHIP, AND THEN I, UH, USED MY TELEPATHY.

HUH? YOU HAVE **TELEPATHY**? I DIDN'T KNOW THAT CHKLITNIANS HAD **TELEPATHY**.

UH. YEAH.

WE DO.

ANYWAY, THANKS!

OOPS. SORRY!
THAT WAS, AN EARTH THING. A KISS. I SHOULDN'T HAVE--

YOUR EARTH CUSTOMS DON'T BOTHER ME.

AND, SERIOUSLY, YOU THINK EARTH IS THE ONLY PLANET THAT'S EVER INVENTED THE TECHNOLOGY OF THE KISS?

OH, SO YOU KISS ON CHKLITN, TOO?

OF COURSE. LET ME SHOW YOU.
GUYS. HATE TO CUT IN, BUT THERE'S COMPANY.

OH. YEAH. SORRY, BOGLEY. KINDA FORGOT YOU WERE THERE. DIDN'T MEAN TO EMBARRASS ANYONE.
NO, I DIDN'T MEAN ME. I MEANT...

...WE GOT COMPANY.

LASERS. BOMBS. BULLETS. EVERY WEAPON THAT ANY SPECIES HAS EVER DEVELOPED, THEY'VE *ALL* PROVED USELESS. THE LEGENDS DON'T HAVE A SINGLE BIT OF ADVICE ON HOW TO SURVIVE AN ATTACK.

ENGINES ARE FREE! WE HAVE **FULL POWER**!
THE PIRATE'S JAMMER FINALLY FADED OUT. LET'S ROAR **OUT** OF HERE!

WE FUNNEL AN ENORMOUS FORTUNE OF FLENNITE INTO THE ENGINES.

FOR A MOMENT THE SHIP TEETERS ON THE EDGE OF REALITY.

AND THEN IT BREAKS THROUGH.

IN THE SPACE OF A HEARTBEAT, WE'VE TRAVELED PAST FOUR GALAXIES. NO SHIP HAS EVER TRAVELED THIS FAST. JUST LIKE THAT, WE BECOME THE FASTEST THINGS IN THE ENTIRE KNOWN HISTORY OF THE UNIVERSE.

EXCEPT FOR THE MORGANTH.
IT'S **STILL** ON US!
HOW IS THIS POSSIBLE! WHAT CAN WE DO?
WE'RE LIKE A **BUG** TO THIS THING!

THAT'S IT! GREAT IDEA, LOWENGEAR!
WHAT? WHAT DID I SAY?

THE MORGANTH IS SO BIG THAT NO MATTER HOW FAST IT IS, IT CAN'T AVOID THE ASTEROIDS IN AN ASTEROID FIELD.

"BUT WE'LL BE A LIKE A MOSQUITO FLYING THROUGH A LOCKED SCREEN DOOR."

SAY AGAIN?
NEVER MIND! NO TIME!
SORAYA! GIVE ME A READING ON THE NEAREST LARGE ASTEROID FIELD!

GOT IT! COURSE PLOTTED!
LET'S GO!

HEY, BENSON. YOU SURE THIS IS A GOOD IDEA?
OH GEEZ. NO, IT ISN'T A GOOD IDEA AT ALL.
BUT SOMETIMES THE ONLY CHOICE YOU HAVE IS TERRIBLE.

UH, BENSON.
THAT WASN'T VERY REASSURING.

SORAYA TAKES THE COMMAND CHAIR AND DRIVES US THROUGH THE ASTEROID FIELD. SHE DRIVES FASTER THAN I COULD, BETTER THAN I COULD, HUMMING TO HERSELF, HEARING MUSIC THAT'S BEYOND ME. SOMETIMES FRIENDS ARE BETTER AT SOMETHING THAN YOU ARE, AND THAT'S FINE. IT'S NOT A CONTEST.
WE SCRAPE PAINT AGAIN AND AGAIN. ONE GOOD HIT AND WE'D BE CRUSHED. IT'S LIKE BEING IN THE MIDDLE OF A POPCORN MACHINE, IF EACH BIT OF POPCORN WAS THE SIZE OF A GARAGE, AND MADE OF ROCK, AND TRAVELING AT FIFTY THOUSAND MILES PER HOUR.

THERE'S NO WAY THE MORGANTH CAN MAKE IT THROUGH THIS!
WE'RE GONNA DIE. **WE'RE GONNA DIE! WE'RE GONNA DIE!**

BUT IT TURNS OUT THERE *IS* A WAY FOR THE MORGANTH TO MAKE IT THROUGH. WE UNDERESTIMATED ITS SHEER POWER. MOST OF THE ASTEROIDS JUST BOUNCE OFF THE BEAST, AS IF THEY WERE NO MORE THAN PAPIER-MÂCHÉ.

AND SOME OF THEM, THE MORGANTH SIMPLY DESTROYS.
OH... **CRAP!**

THE SHEER POWER OF THE CREATURE FOLLOWING US IS WITHOUT PRECEDENT IN THE ENTIRETY OF GALACTIC LORE. I WISH WE COULD TAKE MORE TIME TO ADMIRE IT, EXCEPT IT APPARENTLY WANTS TO EAT US.

A SINGLE STRIKE FROM ONE OF THEM COULD DEVASTATE OUR SHIP, OR EVEN AN ENTIRE CITY. BUT THE CREATURE BARELY SEEMS TO NOTICE.
ARE YOU SERIOUS? WHAT'S THAT THING MADE OF?!?

IT'S TOO FOCUSED ON US.

THE ASTEROIDS AREN'T WORKING! ANY OTHER IDEAS?
LET'S THROW SPRATT OUT! MAYBE THE MORGANTH WILL EAT HIM AND GET SICK?

DO WE HAVE A CLOAKING DEVICE?
MAYBE WE CAN FLY CLOSE TO A BLACK HOLE, AND IT WILL GET SUCKED IN?
IT'S AN ANIMAL, SO MAYBE WE CAN TRICK IT SOMEHOW?

PROJECT A HOLO-ILLUSION OF OUR SHIP GOING IN ANOTHER DIRECTION?
WE DON'T HAVE ANY WAY TO DO THAT, BUT MAYBE WE CAN EJECT THE ENGINE CORE DOWN ITS THROAT, CAUSE A GAMMA RAY EXPLOSION AND DESTROY IT FROM WITHIN?

DON'T THINK WE CAN HURT IT **AT ALL**, NOT WITH THE WAY IT WAS SHRUGGING OFF THOSE ASTEROIDS.
RIGHT. WELL, MAYBE WE CAN...

... LURE IT INTO A SOLAR FLARE, SOMEHOW?
JUST BECAUSE IT CAN SHRUG OFF ASTEROID IMPACTS DOESN'T MEAN IT CAN'T BE **COOKED**.

MAYBE WE DON'T EVEN HAVE TO BEAT IT. IS THERE A WAY WE CAN BLIND IT? IF IT CAN'T **SEE** US, WE COULD JUST LEAVE!
I SUPPOSE IT'S POSSIBLE, BUT WE'RE NOT EVEN SURE IF THAT WOULD HELP.

SOME CREATURES HUNT BY MOVEMENT, OR HEAT SIGNATURES, OR BY SCENT.
THAT'S BAD NEWS, THEN. **SPRATT** STINKS SO BAD THAT THE MORGANTH CAN PROBABLY SCENT HIM FROM A **HUNDRED** PARSECS AWAY.

COULD WE MAYBE USE THE FLENNITE TO AMPLIFY THE QUANTUM PHONE, CREATE A BURST OF SOUND THAT WOULD SCARE THE MORGANTH AWAY?
I DON'T KNOW. MAYBE? WORTH A SHOT. BENSON WAS TELLING ME THAT HE THOUGHT HE COULD AMPLIFY THE LASER PISTOL INTO--
HEY. WHERE **IS** BENSON?

BENSON?
BENSON!

WHAT ARE YOU **DOING**?!!
REMEMBERING WHAT MY DAD TOLD ME.
YOUR DAD TOLD YOU TO GET **EATEN BY A MONSTER**? THAT IS **SO** NOT THE BEST PARENTAL ADVICE!

NO, HE TOLD ME THAT...

... THE IMPORTANT THING WHEN YOU'RE DEALING WITH FEISTY ANIMALS IS TO BE CONFIDENT.

WITH SOME ANIMALS, YOU'RE GOING TO BE THEIR FRIENDS.

WITH OTHERS YOU NEED TO BE STRICT.
BARK BARK!
BARK BARK!

BUT YOU ALWAYS HAVE TO BE THE ONE IN CONTROL.

NEVER THINK FOR A MOMENT THAT YOU'RE *NOT* THE ONE IN CHARGE.

NEVER LET YOUR CONFIDENCE SLIP.

IF *YOU* DON'T DOUBT THAT YOU'RE IN CONTROL, THE ANIMALS WON'T DOUBT IT.

DAD SAID THAT THE MAIN THING IN DEALING WITH ANIMALS IS THE SAME THING AS ANY OTHER PART OF YOUR LIFE.

BELIEVE IN YOURSELF.

WHATEVER. YOU DON'T IMPRESS ME.

STOP!

SIT!

IS IT WORKING?
DO YOU MEAN, IS BENSON SUCCESSFULLY MAKING ME SWEAT BUCKETS?

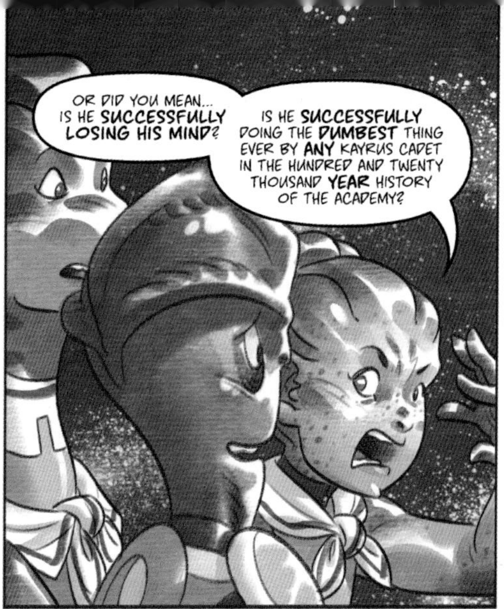
OR DID YOU MEAN... IS HE SUCCESSFULLY LOSING HIS MIND?
IS HE SUCCESSFULLY DOING THE DUMBEST THING EVER BY ANY KAYRUS CADET IN THE HUNDRED AND TWENTY THOUSAND YEAR HISTORY OF THE ACADEMY?

"YES TO ALL OF THOSE!"
STAY.

AND, IF YOU MEAN... IS HE TAMING THE MORGANTH?
I'D HAVE TO SAY... AMAZINGLY... UNBELIEVABLY... INCREDIBLY... YES.

WAIT, ARE YOU TWO HOLDING HANDS?

STAY.
YOU HAVE TO STAY, OKAY?
JUST... STAY.

WHAT'S HE DOING?
IS HE TOO SCARED TO MOVE?

I'D BE TOO SCARED TO MOVE.
I'M NOT EVEN OUT THERE AND I'M TOO SCARED TO MOVE.

IS HE GOING BACK?
WHY'S HE GOING BACK?

GO OUT THERE AND BRING HIM BACK.
ME? I'M NOT GOING OUT THERE TO BRING HIM BACK.

I AM.

HEY. GOOD BOY.
DON'T BE SCARED.

I WAS JUST THINKING...
...I'D NEVER FORGIVE MYSELF IF I DIDN'T...

...DO **THIS**.

EXCUSE ME!
BENSON CHOW!
DO YOU HAVE **SPACE SICKNESS**?

NO. I WANTED TO GO FOR A **RIDE**.

COME **WITH** ME.

WE DIP THROUGH A PLANETARY ATMOSPHERE, WITH THE MORGANTH SHIELDING US FROM THE HEAT, AND WE SKIM AN ALIEN OCEAN, LISTENING TO THE ROARING SURF AND THE CALLS OF ANIMALS THAT NOBODY HAS EVER BEFORE HEARD.

WOW, THAT WAS **FUN**!
THE MOST FUN, **EVER**!
YEAH, IT **WAS**!

WHO SAID THAT?

WAIT... **YOU**?
ME. YES.

YOU CAN **TALK**?
NOT IN ANY LANGUAGE YOU'D UNDERSTAND, NO, BUT I CAN COMMUNICATE TELEPATHICALLY.

OH.

I'M **REALLY** SORRY I CLIMBED YOUR FACE.

NAWW, IT'S ALL GOOD. I HAVEN'T REALLY HAD ANYONE TO TALK TO IN LIKE, TWENTY THOUSAND YEARS, SO I JUST APPRECIATE THE COMPANY.

TWENTY THOUSAND YEARS?
WHAT HAPPENED TO THE OTHERS OF YOUR KIND?

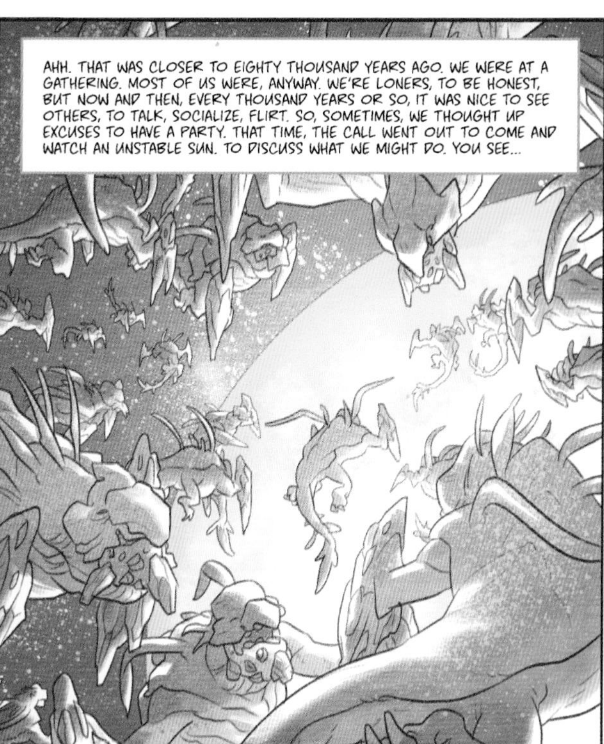
AHH. THAT WAS CLOSER TO EIGHTY THOUSAND YEARS AGO. WE WERE AT A GATHERING. MOST OF US WERE, ANYWAY. WE'RE LONERS, TO BE HONEST, BUT NOW AND THEN, EVERY THOUSAND YEARS OR SO, IT WAS NICE TO SEE OTHERS, TO TALK, SOCIALIZE, FLIRT. SO, SOMETIMES, WE THOUGHT UP EXCUSES TO HAVE A PARTY. THAT TIME, THE CALL WENT OUT TO COME AND WATCH AN UNSTABLE SUN. TO DISCUSS WHAT WE MIGHT DO. YOU SEE...

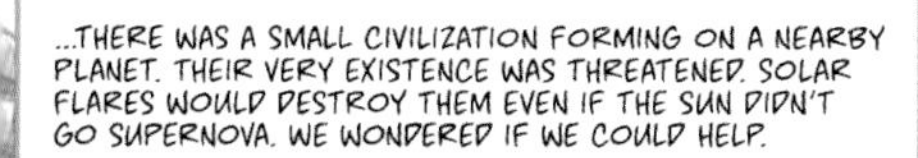
...THERE WAS A SMALL CIVILIZATION FORMING ON A NEARBY PLANET. THEIR VERY EXISTENCE WAS THREATENED. SOLAR FLARES WOULD DESTROY THEM EVEN IF THE SUN DIDN'T GO SUPERNOVA. WE WONDERED IF WE COULD HELP.

WE WERE DOING THE MATH OF PHYSICALLY REMOVING THEIR PLANET FROM ITS ORBIT AND TRANSPORTING IT TO ANOTHER GALAXY WHERE IT COULD ORBIT ANOTHER SUN, WHEN THE SUPERMASSIVE STAR EXPLODED.

IT SHOULDN'T HAVE REACHED CRITICAL MASS SO SOON. IT WAS A ONE-OUT-OF-TRILLIONS POSSIBILITY, BUT... IT HAPPENED.
THE RESULTING EXPLOSION WAS ENOUGH TO TURN EVERYTHING IN THE ENTIRE SOLAR SYSTEM TO VAPOR AND DUST. NOTHING REMAINED. NOT THE PLANETS. NOT THE MOONS. AND NOT MY PEOPLE.

NOTHING REMAINED BUT HEAT, DUST, AND ECHOES.

THE DYING SUN TREMBLED ON THE VERGE OF BECOMING A BLACK HOLE, BUT INSTEAD...
...IT SPURTED OUT A GAS JET THAT VAPORIZED MOST OF THE REST OF MY KIND, WHO WERE HOPING TO COME TO SOME SORT OF RESCUE FROM THE INITIAL EXPLOSION.

OH MAN.
LISTEN, BENSON, SORAYA... YOU NEVER KNOW WHAT LIFE IS GOING TO BRING YOU. LIFE IS PRECIOUS. REMEMBER THAT YOU NEED TO **FIGHT** EVERY DAY, **LAUGH** EVERY DAY, BECAUSE **EVERY** DAY IS ONE **LESS** DAY THAT YOU HAVE.

YOU SOUND PRETTY WISE.

IT'S ONLY BECAUSE I HAVE A DEEP VOICE. I'M MOSTLY JUST REMEMBERING WHAT LITTLE PEG OF THE NEG-LIGHT SYSTEM TOLD ME.
YOU **MET** LITTLE PEG!?

IT WAS SOME THIRTY THOUSAND YEARS AGO, BUT... YES. WE TALKED. WE TRAVELED TO THE CIRCINUS GALAXY AND WATCHED RINGS OF GAS BEING EJECTED, HUNDREDS OF LIGHT YEARS LONG, EATING THEIR WAY THROUGH A METEOR SHOWER IN A SPECTACULAR EXPLOSION OF LIGHTS WITH COLORS THE UNIVERSE HADN'T SEEN IN MILLIONS OF CENTURIES.

WE TOLD GHOST STORIES.

WE TOLD EACH OTHER OUR SECRETS.
WHAT SECRETS?

AH, FOR LITTLE PEG, IT WAS HOW **SCARED** SHE WAS, AT TIMES. HOW SHE SO OFTEN DIDN'T KNOW WHAT TO DO.

SHE FELT THAT WAY?
YES. THAT WAS HER SECRET. OR RATHER, IT WASN'T A SECRET, BECAUSE EVERYONE FEELS THAT WAY. CAN YOU EVEN CONSIDER SOMETHING AS SECRET IF EVERYONE FEELS THE SAME?

AND WHAT WAS **YOUR** SECRET?
MINE? ALMOST THE SAME. IT'S THAT I'M LONELY. FOR TENS OF THOUSANDS OF YEARS, I'VE BEEN ALONE.

AT FIRST, THAT'S THE WAY I WANTED IT. I WAS TOO DEVASTATED BY THE LOSS OF SO MANY OF MY KIND THAT I COULDN'T STAND THE THOUGHT OF GETTING TO KNOW **ANYONE** ELSE, OF RISKING THAT SORROW AGAIN.

BUT I'VE COME TO REALIZE HOW FOOLISH THAT IS. I WAS KEEPING TO MYSELF, OUT OF FEAR OF BEING BY MYSELF. NOT SO VERY SMART. AND IT TOOK ME TENS OF THOUSANDS OF YEARS TO SEE THE FOLLY.

AND TODAY, I SEE THE SOLUTION. THE SAME ONE THAT FIRST ITCHED AT MY BRAIN WHEN I WAS TALKING WITH LITTLE PEG, SO LONG AGO.
YEAH. WHAT'S THAT?

I WANT TO JOIN THE KAYRUS ACADEMY.

THAT'S AWESOME!
YOU CAN BUNK WITH BENSON AND BOGLEY!

YEAH. OKAY, MAYBE A ROOM OF YOUR OWN.

ANYWAY... I **HAVE** TO TELL MY SISTER ALL ABOUT THIS!
A **MORGANTH** IN THE **ACADEMY**?

LORNA! THE MORGANTH IS **INTELLIGENT**! LIKE, **SUPER** INTELLIGENT!
AND HE WANTS TO **JOIN** THE **KAYRUS ACADEMY** AND HE... UH...

WHOA!

ARE YOU TWO **KISSING**?

DAY ONE HUNDRED AND THIRTY-SEVEN: WELCOME, NEW CADET.
AND DO YOU SOLEMNLY SWEAR TO UPHOLD THE HONOR AND TRADITIONS OF THE KAYRUS ACADEMY?
I HEREBY SOLEMNLY SWEAR TO UPHOLD THE...

THIS IS THE GREATEST PUBLICITY COUP IN THE HISTORY OF THE ACADEMY.
A MORGANTH, ALIVE, AND INTELLIGENT, AND A MEMBER OF OUR ACADEMY? THE DONATIONS WILL POUR IN.
PERHAPS YOU CAN EVEN FUND EARTH RESEARCH AGAIN?

OH, PERHAPS. LET'S NOT GET AHEAD OF OURSELVES.
I'D THINK THIS WOULD BE THE **PERFECT** TIME TO, AS YOU SAY, GET AHEAD OF OURSELVES.
WITH THE DONATIONS **ALONE** WE'LL BE ON SOLID FINANCIAL FOOTING, AND THE DONATIONS WILL BE **DWARFED** BY THE VALUE OF THE FLENNITE.

THERE'S ENOUGH FLENNITE TO HERALD A NEW ERA OF SPACE EXPLORATION.
THE KAYRUS ACADEMY WILL BECOME TRULY PERTINENT AGAIN, AND ALL THANKS TO BENSON, THE EARTH BOY.

PLEASE. THE EARTH CHILD WAS JUST A STOWAWAY WHO HAD A RUN OF **LUCK**.
IT WAS SPRATT AND THE OTHERS WHO **INITIATED** THIS GREAT SEARCH.

THEY GOT **LOST**, YOU MEAN, WHILE STEALING ACADEMY PROPERTY AND KIDNAPPING A FELLOW CADET.
WATCH YOUR TONE OF VOICE, PRINN.
JUST BECAUSE THE ACADEMY IS RICH, DOESN'T MEAN WE MIGHT NOT TRIM SOME FAT.

DAY ONE HUNDRED AND FORTY: STORIES FROM STRANGERS.

BENSON CHOW? YEAH. OF **COURSE** WE'RE FRIENDS.
HE'S TOTALLY **ALWAYS** ASKING ME FOR ADVICE.

A FORTUNE. A VAST FORTUNE.
THERE'S NOTHING WE CANNOT DO WITH THIS MUCH WEALTH AT OUR CONTROL.

SO WHAT?
I STILL HATE HIM.

BAKED YOU AN EARTH MEAL! IT'S A **PIZZA**, WITH CAKE FROSTING!

WHY DOES THE MORGANTH KEEP STARING AT THE FLENNITE?

BENSON! SIT OVER **HERE**!

DID YOU HEAR ABOUT HOW BENSON ISN'T **REALLY** FROM EARTH?
REALLY? I **WONDERED**. HE'S TOO ADVANCED FOR THAT SPECIES.

BENSON AND I WERE SECRETLY MARRIED.

DAY ONE HUNDRED AND FORTY-THREE: CULINARY COMPLEXITIES.
BENSON, YOU'RE NEEDED OUTSIDE, NOW! DIRECTOR SQUA-TRONT IS INSISTING THAT--

OUTSIDE! NOW!

SO... IT TURNS OUT THAT MORGANTHS EAT FLENNITE. AND DAVE (THE MORGANTH TOLD ME TO CALL HIM "DAVE" BECAUSE HIS ACTUAL NAME IS UNPRONOUNCEABLE) HAS BEEN THINKING ABOUT DINING ON THE ASTEROID I DISCOVERED.

FOR SOME REASON I'M SUPPOSED TO BE THE ONE WHO SOLVES THE PROBLEM. ON ONE SIDE OF THE ARGUMENT IS DAVE, WHO SAYS HE'S HUNGRY, AND ON THE OTHER SIDE IS THE WHOLE OF THE KAYRUS ACADEMY, WHICH DOESN'T WANT HIM TO EAT THE LARGEST FORTUNE IN THE KNOWN UNIVERSE.

THINGS GET PRETTY HEATED. IT'S INTERESTING TO HEAR CHESHIRE TRANSLATING SEVERAL GALAXIES' WORTH OF CURSE WORDS.
HEY, WHOA!
LET ME... IF YOU'D JUST...
EXCUSE ME... HOLD ON... LET ME...

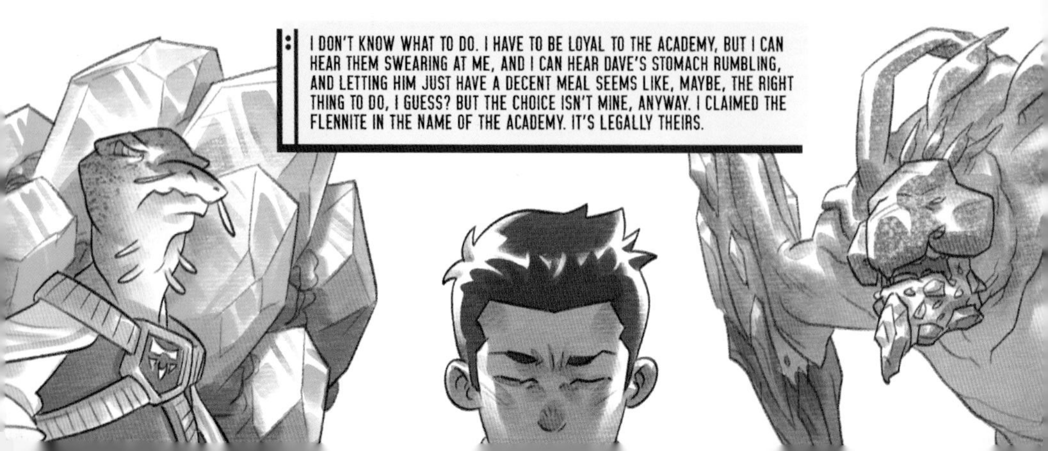
I DON'T KNOW WHAT TO DO. I HAVE TO BE LOYAL TO THE ACADEMY, BUT I CAN HEAR THEM SWEARING AT ME, AND I CAN HEAR DAVE'S STOMACH RUMBLING, AND LETTING HIM JUST HAVE A DECENT MEAL SEEMS LIKE, MAYBE, THE RIGHT THING TO DO, I GUESS? BUT THE CHOICE ISN'T MINE, ANYWAY. I CLAIMED THE FLENNITE IN THE NAME OF THE ACADEMY. IT'S LEGALLY THEIRS.

DAY ONE HUNDRED AND FORTY-FOUR: STRANGERS AND STRANGENESS.
BENSON, CAN YOU PLEEEEASE HELP US WITH THIS NAVIGATION QUESTION?

I CAN'T JUST **STARVE** DAVE. BUT... ARGHH... THERE'S NO WAY TO **SOLVE** THIS!
NOT YOUR CALL, BENSON. THAT FLENNITE ASTEROID BELONGS TO THE ACADEMY, UNFORTUNATELY.

AND, SPECIAL TREAT, WE'LL BE BRINGING IN **BENSON CHOW**, TOMORROW, TO GIVE A LECTURE ON DEEP SPACE EXPLORATION.

HEY, WE NEVER TALKED ABOUT HOW YOUR PEOPLE HAVE TELEPATHY. YOU MUST BE SECRETLY TALKING TO EACH OTHER ALL THE TIME. NEAT!
UMM. YEAH. ABOUT THAT...

I WOULDN'T MESS WITH HIM, IF I WERE YOU. THAT'S **BENSON**'S FRIEND.

MY PEOPLE DON'T HAVE TELEPATHY WITH **EVERYONE**. JUST... **ONE** PERSON. WHOEVER WE FEEL THE, UH, I MEAN... THE **CLOSEST** TO.
HUH? I DON'T GET IT.

THE PIRATES **SHRIEKED** WHEN THEY SAW ME, WITH MY LASER PISTOL IN HAND, AND MY HAIR BILLOWING IN THE ION-SPACE-WIND!
DUDE, YOU DON'T EVEN **HAVE** HAIR.

MAYBE, FOR ONCE, WE CAN SKIP THE REGULATION UNIFORM.

DAY ONE HUNDRED AND FORTY-FIVE: THE PAPERS.
IT IS WITH GREAT HONOR, AND EXTREME JOY, THAT I PRESENT BENSON CHOW WITH HIS UNFORTUNATELY **LONG**-DELAYED OFFICIAL ENROLLMENT PAPERS.

NOW, NORMALLY WE DON'T MAKE SUCH A **SHOW** OF THIS, BUT WE FELT THE CIRCUMSTANCES RATED THIS GRAND FÊTE.

THERE! I'VE ADDED MY NAME TO THE PAPERS, AND, AS SOON AS BENSON SIGNS, WE WILL **LEGALLY** WELCOME HIM TO THE ARMS OF THE KAYRUS ACADEMY, AS WE HAVE **ALREADY** EXTENDED OUR HEARTS.

HE'S **REALLY** LAYING IT ON, OUT THERE.
IT'S NICE, IN A WEIRD WAY. AFTER ALL I'VE BEEN THROUGH, IT'S GRATIFYING TO HAVE SOMEONE BE SO... PROUD OF ME.
WELL, HE **DOES** LOVE A SHOW.

SURE. IF **PRIDE** IS WHAT IT IS.
HUH?

I'M JUST SAYING THAT THERE ARE THOSE OF US WHO DIDN'T HAVE TO SIGN ANY **LEGAL** DOCUMENTS TO MAKE YOU FEEL WELCOME.
IF THIS ACADEMY HAS TAUGHT YOU ANYTHING, IT'S TO LOOK **BELOW** THE SURFACE LEVEL, AND TO SEE WHAT'S HAPPENING **BENEATH** THE WATER.

CAN'T **WAIT** FOR YOU TO SIGN, BENSON!

HURRY! **HURRY**!

HERE'S YOUR PEN. SIGN **FIRST**, AND THEN A SPEECH.
I'M SURE YOU HAVE SO MUCH TO SAY! BUT... SIGN **FIRST**.

WAIT A SECOND.
I'M NOT CURRENTLY A LEGAL STUDENT.
I HAVE **NO** LEGAL STANDING IN THE ACADEMY.

"THAT MEANS THAT... WHEN I CLAIMED THE FLENNITE IN THE NAME OF THE **ACADEMY**... THERE WAS NO **LEGALLY** BINDING RELATIONSHIP.
"WHICH **IN TURN** MEANS OWNERSHIP OF A BILLION TRILLION DOLLARS WORTH OF FLENNITE REVERTS BACK TO THE PERSON WHO DISCOVERED IT."

ME.

CHESHIRE, FILE A LEGAL CLAIM.
I, BENSON CHOW, HEREBY DECLARE MYSELF AS SOLE OWNER OF THE FLENNITE ASTEROID I DISCOVERED.

THERE. THAT'S SETTLED. AND NOW, I GUESS I'LL SIGN THIS ENROLLMENT FORM.
IT'S HONESTLY THE BIGGEST HONOR OF MY LIFE TO BECOME AN OFFICIAL KAYRUS ACADEMY CADET.

THANK YOU, SIR.
HERE'S YOUR PEN BACK.

CLAP
CLAP
CLAP
CLAP

CLAP
CLAP
CLAP
CLAP
CLAP
CLAP
CLAP
CLAP
CLAP
CLAP
CLAP
CLAP
CLAP

HEY, DAVE! YOU **HUNGRY**?
HONESTLY, BENSON... I'M KINDA **STARVING**.

WELL, THE FLENNITE'S LEGALLY **MINE**, NOW.
HAVE AS MUCH AS YOU'D LIKE.

DAY ONE HUNDRED AND FORTY-SIX: THE BATHROOM BREAK.

WAKE UP!

AN INCREDIBLE DAY, TODAY.
HUH? WHAT'S UP?
GET DRESSED! GET DRESSED! HURRY!

A LIFE-CHANGING DAY, REALLY. AND NOT JUST MY LIFE. EVERYONE'S.
BENSON! THERE YOU ARE! HURRY!

I WENT TO BED WITH EVERYONE TALKING ABOUT WHAT A FOOL I WAS, LETTING DAVE EAT A HUGE AMOUNT OF FLENNITE, WHICH FUELS ALL THE MODIFIED ALCUBIERRE DRIVE ENGINES, AND WHICH IS ALMOST THE MOST EXPENSIVE SUBSTANCE IN THE UNIVERSE.

THE ONLY THING MORE EXPENSIVE IS TRIBIUM, AN INCREDIBLY RARE ORE THAT, WHEN MIXED WITH OTHER METALS, BECOMES THE ONLY KNOWN SUBSTANCE IN THE ENTIRE UNIVERSE THAT CAN WITHSTAND THE RIGORS OF FTL SPACETIME-FOLDING FLIGHT.

A FEW OUNCES OF TRIBIUM IS ENOUGH TO FORTIFY A GRAND CRUISER. UNTIL THIS MORNING, EVERYBODY THOUGHT THAT TRIBIUM WAS A NATURALLY OCCURRING, FINITE, MINERAL.

UNTIL DAVE *POOPED*, THAT IS.

PRINN, WHAT'S HAPPENING?
WHAT **IS** THIS?

POOP, I GUESS. YOUR MORGANTH FRIEND **EATS** FLENNITE AND **POOPS** TRIBIUM.
THIS REWRITES HALF OF WHAT WE KNOW ABOUT MORGANTHS, AND FLENNITE, AND TRIBIUM.
THIS... THIS REWRITES HALF OF WHAT WE KNOW ABOUT THE **UNIVERSE**.

"THIS OPENS UP THE UNIVERSE EVEN MORE. **FLEETS** OF NEW SHIPS CAN BE BUILT. BUILT **AND** POWERED."

AND IT'S ALL THANKS TO **YOU**, BENSON.
ALL THANKS TO WHAT YOU'VE DONE.

AND JUST LIKE THAT, DAD... I BECAME THE RICHEST PERSON IN THE WHOLE GALACTIC FEDERATION. ALL THANKS TO ASTEROIDS AND FRIENDSHIP AND POOP.
THAT'S AN UNLIKELY COMBINATION. BUT, JUST SO I UNDERSTAND, HOW MUCH MONEY DID YOU SAY YOU HAVE, NOW?

HONESTLY? ENOUGH TO BUY AND SELL GALAXIES.

"I'VE ALREADY STARTED RENOVATING AND EXPANDING THE KAYRUS ACADEMY, WITH NOTHING BUT THE MEREST **FRACTION** OF MY MONEY.

"I'VE ALSO FUNDED SCOUTING MISSIONS TO... WELL... EVERYWHERE. ALL THE BOUNDLESS REACHES OF THE UNIVERSE THAT ARE STILL OUT THERE WAITING.

"AND... I'M REALLY PROUD OF THIS... I'VE STARTED SCHOLARSHIP PROGRAMS FOR THE CITIZENS OF **THOUSANDS** OF PREVIOUSLY NEGLECTED PLANETS LIKE EARTH."

DAY ONE HUNDRED AND NINETY-NINE: CAN'T BELIEVE EVERYTHING IS HAPPENING SO FAST. YESTERDAY WAS THE RIBBON-CUTTING CEREMONY FOR THE KAYRUS OUTPOST I FUNDED ON EARTH.
KAYRUS ACADEMY
Look farther. Go farther.

IT'S NOT JUST A DREAM FOR OTHERS FROM EARTH TO BECOME KAYRUS CADETS ANYMORE; IT'S A REAL OPPORTUNITY.
KAYRUS ADMISSIONS

AND, HERE AT KAYRUS, I'M DOING THINGS FROM THE SMALL SCALE, SUCH AS BUILDING DETENTION ROOMS...

TO EXPANDING THE SCOPE OF THE CLASSROOMS...

AND HELPING SPEED THE DEVELOPMENT OF SPECIES ON THREATENED WORLDS, WHILE PRESERVING THE WILDERNESS AREAS THROUGHOUT KNOWN GALAXIES.

... YOU SHOULD HAVE BEEN WORKING FOR **HIS**.

DAY TWO HUNDRED AND FIFTY-TWO: THE SHIPS ARE COMING IN. SORAYA AND I ARE SPENDING THE DAY WATCHING THE NEW CADETS ARRIVING IN PORT.

WITH THE FUNDS I'VE MADE AVAILABLE TO KAYRUS, THE RECRUITS ARE COMING FROM A FAR WIDER RANGE OF GALAXIES. IT'S A PERFECT START FOR MY SECOND YEAR OF RANGER TRAINING, KNOWING THAT I PLAYED SOME SMALL PART IN BRINGING IN THESE CADETS, MANY OF WHOM WOULDN'T HAVE OTHERWISE BEEN GIVEN A CHANCE. THERE'S ALL THESE NEW PEOPLE WITH A DESIRE TO EXPLORE, AND TO MAKE THE UNIVERSE A BETTER PLACE. IT'S EXCITING. I'M ACTUALLY SHIVERING.

WOW! BENSON! THERE HE IS!
IT'S ACTUALLY **HIM**!
IT'S **BENSON CHOW**!
LOOKS LIKE YOU'RE GOING TO HAVE TO SAY A FEW WORDS. MAYBE TELL THEM ABOUT PIZZA, OR ABOUT HOW LOUD BOGLEY SNORES?

I FEEL SILLY, PRETENDING TO BE SOME CELEBRITY, BUT SORAYA SAYS IT'S IMPORTANT TO INSPIRE OTHERS. I GUESS THAT'S TRUE, BUT IT'S DIFFICULT TO TRULY BELIEVE THAT *DRRG* OF PENN OR LITTLE *PEG* OF THE NEG-LIGHT SYSTEM EVER FELT LIKE THIS.
WELCOME TO KAYRUS! GREAT TO SEE YOU!

ANY ADVICE YOU CAN GIVE US?
SURE. OF COURSE.
WHAT YOU NEED TO REMEMBER IS...

... YOU'RE PART OF KAYRUS, NOW.
DON'T BE CONCERNED WITH HOW SOMEONE **LOOKS**. PAY ATTENTION TO WHERE THEY'RE **LOOKING**.
AND DON'T CARE TOO MUCH ABOUT WHERE THEY'VE **BEEN**.

LOOK TO SEE WHERE THEY'RE **GOING**.

EARTH BOY™

SKETCHBOOK

NOTES BY RON CHAN

BENSON

Below are some explorations of Benson's design, and the very first drawings to be made for *Earth Boy*. Though Benson changes outfits throughout the book, red was often his color of choice if out of uniform.

SORAYA, LORNA, AND BOGLEY

The Kayrus student uniform actually originated from my initial drawings of Lorna and Soraya below. At first, I drew the twins in similar outfits to connect just the two of them, but later decided to base everyone's uniforms off their look!

ACADEMY INSTRUCTORS AND STUDENTS

Various designs of supporting and background characters. You can see here that my first drawing of Spratt didn't have the more bird-like chest of his final design, and that Lowengear, at one point, had uniform sleeves that didn't make it into the book.

BENSON'S DAD & KENJI

Kenji's design is very loosely based on a close friend of mine from childhood, and Benson's dad very much looks like my dad!

Above, we have some very loose shape explorations for Kayrus inhabitants.

TEST PAGE

This was the test page used to get *Earth Boy* off the ground, showing Benson arriving at Kayrus. Originally, I imagined using more limited colors for the backgrounds as seen here, but later decided to go with fully rendered color.

SPECULATIVE FICTION FROM

dark horse originals

"Unique creators with unique visions."—MIKE RICHARDSON, PUBLISHER

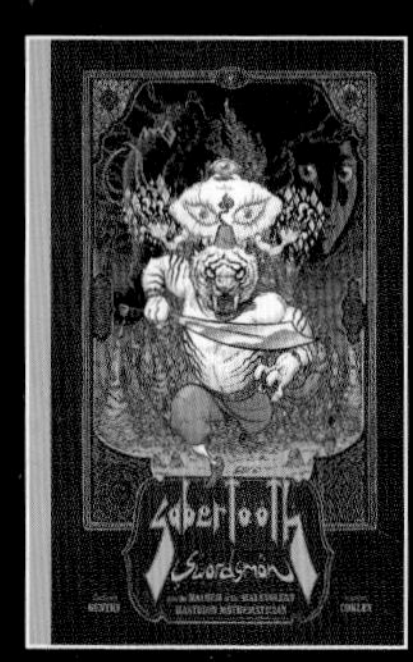

SABERTOOTH SWORDSMAN

Damon Gentry and Aaron Conley

Granted the form of the Sabertooth Swordsman by the Cloud God of Sasquatch Mountain, a simple farmer embarks on a treacherous journey to the Mastodon's fortress!

ISBN 978-1-61655-176-6 | $17.99

PIXU: THE MARK OF EVIL

Gabriel Bá, Becky Cloonan, Vasilis Lolos, and Fábio Moon

This gripping tale of urban horror follows the lives of five lonely strangers who discover a dark mark scrawled on the walls of their building. As the walls come alive, everyone is slowly driven mad, stripped of free will, leaving only confusion, chaos, and eventual death.

ISBN 978-1-61655-813-0 | $14.99

SACRIFICE

Sam Humphries, Dalton Rose, Bryan Lee O'Malley, and others

What happens when a troubled youth is plucked from modern society and sent on a psychedelic journey into the heart of the Aztec civilization—one of the greatest and most bloodthirsty times in human history?

ISBN 978-1-59582-985-6 | $19.99

DE:TALES

Fábio Moon and Gabriel Bá

Brimming with all the details of human life, Moon and Bá's charming stories move from the urban reality of their home in São Paulo to the magical realism of their Latin American background. Named by *Booklist* as one of the 10 Best Graphic Novels of 2010.

ISBN 978-1-59582-557-5 | $19.99

MIND MGMT OMNIBUS

Matt Kindt

This globe-spanning tale of espionage explores the adventures of a journalist investigating the mystery of a commercial flight where everyone aboard loses their memories. Each omnibus volume collects two volumes of the Eisner Award–winning series!

VOLUME 1: THE MANAGER AND THE FUTURIST
ISBN 978-1-50670-460-9 | $24.99

VOLUME 2: THE HOME MAKER AND THE MAGICIAN
ISBN 978-1-50670-461-6 | $24.99

VOLUME 3: THE ERASER AND THE IMMORTALS
ISBN 978-1-50670-462-3 | $24.99

AVAILABLE AT YOUR LOCAL COMICS SHOP OR BOOKSTORE

To find a comics shop near you, visit comicshoplocator.com • For more information or to order direct, visit DarkHorse.com